JOEY WILDE:

SECRETS IN THE CITY

Joey Wilde:
Secrets of the City

A tale of a young gay man in the city.

Jonathan Blackwell

Published in the U.S.A. by Ingram Spark

Edited by Gregory W. Vigue, J.D.

ISBN: 979-8-9995321-1-4

Library of Congress Control Number: 2025914981

Secrets

What makes something a secret? Is it something kept from others out of fear of exposure, or is it intended to create intrigue by deliberately hiding it, making it difficult to uncover?

Secrets are intertwined with our daily lives, sometimes delicate enough to break with a gentle tug, and at other times, like heavy chains, we silently carry. We discover them by chance or hold them close, protecting their significance. The essence of a secret is uncertain—its existence balancing between revealing and hiding, trust and betrayal. As you read these pages, think about: what secrets do you hold, and what are the sacrifices involved in keeping them?

What you find might surprise you.

~Jonathan

CONTENTS

CHAPTER 1
A Fresh Perspective

The early months of 1988 had arrived in Toronto, Canada, without a token celebration by one of Toronto's newest residents. Joey Wilde took a bite of a slice of pizza he bought at a small store on Yonge Street; the winter wind off Lake Ontario turned his cheeks red. He headed toward the lake and turned left onto The Esplanade, where his condo topped a wedge-shaped building.

The condo he inherited from David, a gay client of his, was a three-bedroom, two-bath penthouse with spectacular views. Situated just two blocks from the waterfront, it was prime real estate.

Joey was neither from Toronto nor Canadian. He was from a small town in Maine, in the United States. After two years in the Navy, he moved to Key West, Florida, and became an escort—although not in the way one might think. He didn't provide sex to his only client. Instead, he offered companionship and massages to a man who was HIV positive. Joey developed a massage business, catering to gay men.

Their professional relationship lasted for six months before David contracted AIDS, which led to his death. With no family, he left everything to Joey, whom he both loved and considered his only friend. As a real estate attorney, David built substantial wealth. After paying the lawyers, Joey had about 5 million dollars, two properties, and two cars—a Mercedes-Benz and a Ferrari. He sold the Benz and the house, retaining only the condo where he lives and the sports car.

Key West was a bittersweet experience for him. Initially, he drove to the island in an old Ford Van, in which he slept. As he met people, made friends, and became self-employed, he fell for a doctor. Eventually, they moved in together in a house purchased by his lover, JJ, but the relationship didn't last long. JJ stepped out on Joey, which ended the relationship. This inspired him to relocate to Toronto.

Joey left Key West feeling financially secure and having two new friends, Sandy and Shayne. Sandy was a brown-haired, brown-eyed lesbian from Illinois, and Shayne was an attractive gay man with chiseled features, short blond hair, and blue eyes. Shayne was also from Toronto, but chose to stay in Miami Beach with his new lover.

Joey entered the large condominium through the front door. The building featured Art Deco and Beaux-Arts influences and had a unique flatiron shape. The area around the front desk reflected the exterior style, with a polished marble floor extending toward a row of elevators.

Joey waved to a man behind the desk, who returned the gesture before focusing on arranging accommodations to meet the various needs of the residents. He intended to rely on the concierge to help book restaurants and cultural events around the city. Having been in Toronto for less than a month, Joey hadn't explored the city's offerings, or its gay community, bars, clubs, and other venues. His knowledge was limited to what was advertised in Toronto's NOW Magazine, a publication he noticed had a very risqué personals section and was easily found at many city locations. If he chose to reopen his massage service, he might advertise in NOW Magazine.

He stepped into one of the elevators reserved for the two penthouses. He punched in an access code, and the elevator whisked him up the 33 stories, opening directly into his living room.

Joey walked to the kitchen and tossed the shopping bag he carried onto his bar. From the kitchen, he had a magnificent view of the city through floor-to-ceiling windows that ran the entire width of the apartment.

He opened the bag and took out the new sheets he purchased from Holt Renfrew, Toronto's upscale department store. Joey redesigned the master bedroom with fresh sheets, a duvet, and pillowcases. It felt creepy sleeping on the linens of a deceased person, even if they looked brand new. He discarded the old ones. The new sheets were for the guest room.

Joey kept David's furniture and artwork; they were of high quality and tasteful, especially the antique Asian bust, which he assumed was worth a great deal of money. David wouldn't buy a replica or a fake.

He wandered into his bedroom and stripped off his clothes, preparing to shower. Next to the queen-size bed were built-in closets with doors made from dark, rich mahogany, a mirror set into one of them. Joey stood in front of it, looking at his body. The deep tan that he maintained in Key West was fading.

Joey's chest, lats, and biceps were still muscular. He ran his hands over his chest and then down his stomach, where his six-pack abs were prominent. Joey showed not a hint of fat anywhere.

Joey's pride was his thick, sun-bleached hair that flowed over his shoulders and down his back, resembling a rock star. It made him curious about others' impressions when he would cruise in his Camaro or Ferrari during the upcoming summer. He sighed and ran his hand through his hair.

Standing in the afternoon light, Joey let the distant hum of the city remind him how far he had come. The past month shifted beneath his feet like the tides off the coast of Florida, with each decision creating ripples. He moved through the penthouse, its quiet luxury contrasting with the uncertainty that filled so much of his life. The sheets, the furniture, even the city skyline—all of it signaled new beginnings. Yet Joey was aware of the echoes tugging at his memory, especially how Key West had changed him.

He recalled the journey that had led him to that point, prior to the heartbreak, the inheritance, and the Toronto skyline. His old Ford van—his first true sense of freedom—served as both sanctuary and starting point. Joey remembered the restless feeling as he headed south, crossing state borders in search of warmth, both physical and emotional.

He closed his eyes for a moment, recalling the anticipation that filled him the moment Florida's palms began to line the road, the promise of something unknown just ahead.

Joey showered and dressed, then returned to the kitchen where he opened the fridge and examined its contents. He still hadn't done any proper shopping, so there wasn't much to nibble on, let alone to eat for a meal. He would be dining out again. The question was where?

He learned that one of the gay areas was in and around the streets of Church and Wellesley. The area was home to restaurants, clubs, and discos. Who knew what else might be hiding there?

Joey sank onto the sectional sofa and reached for the NOW Magazine on the coffee table. He hoped it might reveal a culinary spot worth exploring. His eyes landed on a small, quarter-page ad at the top corner of page 6, for an Italian restaurant called Dino's. Reading the advertisement, he thought it was perfect—an informal, local spot with two dollar signs suggesting it wasn't fancy. The weekly special was Chicken Parmigiana for $2.99. Joey decided to give it a try. He also figured he wouldn't need reservations, so he didn't bother calling Charlie, the concierge.

The restaurant was located on Church Street, a considerable distance away, so he would need to take a cab. He wasn't driving either of his remaining cars, as it was the middle of winter. The Benz had been sold before he had arrived in Toronto. He kept the Ferrari and the Camaro covered in the underground garage of the condominium for safety. The city also had excellent public transportation, including the Toronto Subway, which could take him to most places. If he didn't use the subway, he took a taxi. Buses were out of the question as he didn't like them.

He checked himself in the mirror again. The white shirt looked great underneath the leather jacket he was wearing, showing just enough of his muscular physique. He had chosen faded jeans with black leather boots and a matching black studded leather belt to complete the ensemble. Satisfied, he checked his wallet to make sure he had enough cash for the evening, because he might check out a club after dinner, and there was one that interested him. Chaps, advertised as a simple bar where gay men gathered, was just what Joey was looking for. He would forgo the nightclub dance scene for now.

Shayne deeply missed Joey and wondered why he hadn't called after leaving Key West so suddenly. He understood his friend's departure and couldn't fault him. Shayne thought Joey might have gone to Toronto, where his inheritance awaited, but wasn't sure if he had collected it or decided to stay. He hoped the latter, mainly because things were tough in Miami Beach. His former sugar daddy, Jefferson, for whom he worked as an escort, lost his job, leaving Shayne without his escort position. Although he still lived in Jefferson's condo, he planned to return to Toronto as soon as possible. Shayne wished he knew Joey's location, as it would be nice to have a friend to hang out with upon his return. Currently, his only remaining friend in the city was Claire, a lesbian high school graduate with whom he had grown up. He had asked her to move with him to Key West, but she declined, opting instead to attend university. His immediate family-lived in Mississauga, just south of Toronto. None of them knew he was homosexual, but he suspected that his mother might. Mothers always seemed to know.

It had been nearly a month before he finally had enough of the abuse, packed his bags, and left Miami Beach without even saying goodbye to Jefferson. Their relationship had become strained after Jefferson lost his job, and he grew increasingly abusive toward

Shayne, blaming him for his unemployment. He needed to find some way to contact his friend Joey, but so far, he had no idea how. For the time being, he would stay with Claire, who had delayed starting school because she had found a job as a waitress in the gay area of Toronto at a restaurant called Dino's. She claimed she just wasn't ready to pursue furthering her education. She was young, and there were too many more fun things to do in the city. School was nothing more than a distraction.

The drive home would take Shayne twenty-two hours, so he decided to stop along the way. Initially, he had the idea of stopping in Illinois to see Sandy, but the detour was well out of the way and would add hours to the trip. Also, he couldn't be sure she was still there, because he couldn't get in touch with her either. No one was answering the phone at her parents' house. He decided to stop at a hotel in the Carolinas somewhere along I-95.

He had left one morning while Jefferson was out job hunting. He left a note saying he wanted to go back home and wished Jefferson the best, which was more than he deserved. Jefferson's verbal assaults hurt Shayne deeply, and he believed the change would do him good. He didn't look back as he drove north out of Florida.

Joey stepped out of the cab and onto a wet Church Street, drizzling rain falling onto his leather jacket. He moved quickly onto the sidewalk and under the awning of a bookstore that advertised adult toys, movie booths, and books at discounted prices. Inside, he could see men meandering about and assumed that they were cruising more than they were shopping.

He pulled the collar up around his neck and cursed himself for not bringing an umbrella, but it had not been raining when he left The Esplanade, and the weather station had forecast snow, not this mixture of sleet and snow that was changing into steady rain.

He took a moment and peered into the adult bookstore. Besides the men who were cruising one another, he could see shelves of VHS tapes sorted with labels straight, gay, and bisexual hung on them. Behind the counter were some of the more expensive toys, as well as bottles of poppers, and he could make out the brands Rush, Bolt, and Thrust, among others. He had never used them, but many of his clients did. The liquid in the small jars gave whoever sniffed it a powerful and short-lasting high. Mainly used during sex, it was preferred by men who indulged in anal sex, including fisting. A practice that Joey had no interest in pursuing.

He found none of the men attractive and turned to leave. Dino's was just a couple of storefronts down the street. He was hungry, and a hot meal sounded delicious as he stood in the cold Toronto evening. The leather jacket he wore wasn't enough to fend off the winter chill. He needed to buy a lined coat designed for the harsh northern winters. He had his ski jacket, but it wasn't sexy, so he left it in the closet.

As Joey walked, he became aware of men passing by him, actively cruising him but not daring to approach. Before any of them could do so, he arrived at Dino's and stepped inside into the warmth, the aroma of Italian food filling his nostrils. He walked up to a pedestal where a sign read "Please wait to be seated," and picked up one of the menus stacked next to it. Before he had a chance to browse through it, a young girl appeared.

"Table for one?" She asked with a smile.

"Yes, please," Joey said, taking in the girl. She wore a waitress's outfit in the style and colors of Italy—a short dress and matching top in green, red, and white. She had short blond hair with brown eyes that sat a little closer together than usual, and her nose was small, like a button sewn onto her face between her eyes. She was also short, no more than 5'5", including the heels she wore.

She led him to a table that overlooked the street.

"Will this do?"

"Perfect," Joey replied, sitting down.

My name is Claire, and I will be your waitress. Would you like something to drink?

"I'm Joey," he replied. "I'll have a Jack and Ginger, please. Light on the Jack Daniels." Joey flashed a perfect smile, and Claire took notice. Not because she found Joey particularly attractive, but she knew of a friend who would consider Joey drop-dead gorgeous. Unfortunately, he wasn't here but would be soon.

"Coming right up!" Claire said cheerfully and hurried away.

Joey believed he had chosen a good place to eat. The chicken parmesan was delicious, as was the service Claire provided. He left her a $30.00 tip, ten times the cost of his meal, and then left the restaurant.

CHAPTER 2
Chaps

Shayne pulled into a Howard Johnson's hotel and restaurant just outside of Fayetteville, its orange roof shining in the setting sun. He left very early in the morning and was tired. Thirteen hours on the road was enough for the day. The hotel and restaurant combination was perfect for what he was looking for: affordable lodging for the night, and the attached restaurant would provide him with meals.

It was his first time at Howard Johnson's restaurant, and it met his expectations. Burgers and sandwiches, as well as typical American desserts, were available at affordable prices. He sat on a stool at the countertop, which looked out through a transparent partition into the kitchen, where a few people scrambled to cook the meals. There was just one other man who sat two seats down from him. Shayne gave him the once-over and decided that he looked to be in his thirties, attractive, dressed casually in jeans and a polo shirt. His brown hair was collar-length, and from the quick look at his face when they exchanged a greeting, his eyes were brown. It didn't take long before they were chatting with one another, and Shayne had moved to sit next to him.

"So, I'm heading home to Toronto after spending the season in Key West," Shayne said, dipping a French fry into a pool of ketchup on this plate. He didn't need to mention the disaster in Miami to a stranger.

"Cool. I was just in Miami visiting a friend on South Beach. It was ok."

"Just ok?"

"Well, I found it dirty and run down. I guess I had expected more when he had asked me to visit."

Shayne immediately picked up on the word "he." "What did the two of you do while you were there?"

"The usual touristy things, I guess. The beach, nightclubs, and bars. That sort of thing." He replied. "By the way, I'm Jeff."

"Shayne. Nice to meet you. I know the beach a little. Which bars did you go to?" Shayne asked, trying not to sound nosy.

" We went to Uncle Charlie's in the Hamlet in Coconut Grove. They were cool."

"Bingo." Shayne thought. Both establishments were gay, and he spent more than once enjoying them with and without Jefferson. "I've been to both of those quite a few times."

"Oh?" Jeff replied.

It seemed to Shayne that Jeff was making the connection as well. He was attracted to Jeff and was hoping it was mutual. It would make the evening more entertaining than watching TV and trying to fall asleep. Twenty minutes later, in Jeff's room. Jeff's eager tongue licked Shayne's naked, muscular body, paying special attention to his belly button and his flat stomach.

"You are so fucking sexy," Jeff said, kissing the inside of Shayne's thighs, teasing his balls with the tip of his tongue. "You smell so good."

Jeff's actions were making Shayne moan, his excitement building. It had been weeks since he felt the passionate touch of a man; Jefferson was the last, but all of that lust had fallen into the abyss. This was rekindling that old spark, and he was enjoying it immensely.

"Suck on them," Shayne begged his lover, grasping Jeff's head in his hands and moving his mouth to his man sac.

Jeff complied and then moved upward, bathing the underside of Shayne's rock-hard cock in glistening moisture. Reaching the head, he let it slip between his teeth and began to gently suck Shayne's throbbing cock. Shayne rotated and moved his hips, attempting to force his ever-hardening dick deeper into his mouth. Jeff was an expert cocksucker, and it was ecstasy for Shayne. Now, Shayne took over as the top.

He pulled Jeff up and plunged his tongue into his mouth, exploring it while reaching down to fondle his erect cock. At a good six inches, it was not as large as Shayne's. Releasing Jeff from the kiss, he pushed him onto his back, grabbed his ankles, and then stopped. Condom, he reminded himself, and took the packet he had gotten from his wallet and tore it open, sliding the latex over his erect member. The protective sheath had come pre-lubricated, negating the need for additional creams or gels. Shayne placed the head of his cock, touching Jeff's orifice, and pushed it inside, causing Jeff to groan loudly.

"It's fucking huge." He said, grimacing.

"You can handle it," Shayne replied. "Relax." He pushed another two inches into the tight hole, stretching it further.

"Oh my God!" Jeff was in pain that was slowly giving way to pleasure with each additional inch that Shayne pushed into him.

With a grunt, Shayne buried his cock fully into Jeff's ass, his balls touching Jeff's ass cheeks. Shayne withdrew, then pushed it back in, his balls once again slapping Jeff's round, inviting ass.

"Oh, fuck yeah, baby!" Jeff cried, moving his hips in a circular motion to enhance the feelings.

Shayne was in ecstasy. He positioned Jeff's legs up and over his shoulders, which allowed for full penetration, and the wild-man ferocity of his thrusts, his body slapping loudly against Jeff.

Satisfied, Shayne quickly flipped over the smaller man and placed him on his hands and knees, then forced his head down into the pillow. He grasped Jeff's waist and continued his hard, deep fucking, slapping his cheeks, leaving light red marks on them. Jeff, in turn, pushed back to take Shayne's cock deeper, although it was already completely buried with each thrust that Shayne made.

Shayne and Jeff neared climax, while Jeff frantically beat his cock with his hand, and Shayne yelled, "I'm going to cum."

He pounded Jeff's ass as hard as he could, then, halting with his cock buried deep, waves of orgasmic pleasure coursed through his body. Jeff came seconds later, his sperm erupting and covering the bed.

Shayne collapsed on top of Jeff, breathing heavily. "That was awesome."

Jeff agreed. "And I thought that my lover was good in bed. You are miles better than he is."

Shayne suddenly lost complete interest in Jeff. The man was cheating on his lover, and it made him sick to his stomach. He got up and dressed, gave him some lame excuse, and went back to his room, where he showered and went to bed.

Chaps was not a large establishment, and Joey was surprised to find that it featured male strippers. As he walked in, he was met by a doorman who asked him if he was a new dancer. Joey had said, "No, just a customer like everyone else," and then entered the dimly lit room, the stage the only thing brightly lit by the spotlights illuminating the dancer on the stage.

The young man had a muscular body with hair similar in length to Joey's that he whipped about his head as he danced. He thought back to when he and Shayne had entered the best body contest at One Saloon in Key West. That was only a few months ago, but a great deal had transpired since then.

Two bars served the dozen or so men. Some were at the bars, which had no seating; a few were up by the stage, affording them a clear and unobstructed view of the naked dancer. The rest were sitting at tables placed around the space. Joey also saw three more dancers who were giving lap dances to men, grinding their naked crotches inches from the customer's face, but careful not to get too close. Touching of any kind was prohibited, as indicated by signs posted on the walls and illuminated with small lights.

Joey also noticed that the majority of the men in Chaps were mature and appeared to be businessmen. He seemed to be the youngest in the crowd, and it wasn't long before he was approached.

"Are you one of the dancers?" A bald man asked him. He was slightly slurring, apparently from the martini that he held in his hand.

"No," Joey replied. "Just a customer."

"You should be." The man said, taking one last look at Joey, then stumbling off.

Joey shook his head and then decided to leave. No one in the bar looked appetizing.

Outside, the rain turned into fluffy snow that drifted down and stuck to the sidewalk. The temperature had dropped significantly, and the wet street had turned to a thin coat of ice that was now being covered by the fresh snow. A large truck with a plow attached to it passed by, spreading a mixture of sand and salt onto the road. It hit a puddle that had yet to completely freeze, sending a spray of water that nearly hit Joey. He dodged it and began to look for a cab to hail. Being alone on such a nasty night was no fun, so he decided to head home.

As a cab pulled up, he noticed a magazine rack and opened it, taking the latest copy of NOW magazine and tucked it into his leather jacket. He would at least have something to read before going to bed.

He also had the cab stop at a Beer Store near his condo and ran in to grab a case of Molson Golden. He found it odd that one had to purchase beer in specified stores instead of the local grocery or corner store—one of many things he was discovering since moving to Canada.

Back in his apartment, he put a dozen bottles in the empty refrigerator and took one that he opened. The rest of the box he put into the pantry, which housed the stacked washer and dryer. He took the bottle and walked to the large windows of the living room, and looked out across the lit-up skyline of Toronto. Unlike Key West, the city had its own magic and allure, and Joey found it fascinating. If only he had someone to share it with. Even David would have been some form of company.

He wondered about Shayne and how he was doing. He hadn't been able to get his new Miami phone number because Shayne didn't know it himself. Everything happened quickly for both of them. Problems with JJ had developed over several weeks, but the breakup occurred in just two days, and Joey's decision to leave was sudden. Shayne took longer, and he didn't depart at the same time as Joey. Joey was deeply torn inside and failed to reach out to his friend. All that mattered was escaping Key West and JJ as quickly as possible.

Joey sat down and opened the magazine. NOW magazine was an independent publication similar to The Rag, which was based in Key West; both publications featured articles that focused on conflict and stories of the debauchery prominent in their respective cities. Joey thought that most of these stories were made up by writers sitting in small offices, dreaming up tales to attract the magazine's readers. He flipped through its pages before landing on the classifieds section. He began to read through them and came across the personals. Most of the ads were for people selling sex, although they were disguised as offering other things, such as companionship, body rubs, and a few that blatantly searched for an older, well-off man or woman. It seemed to Joey that it wasn't only gay men advertising in NOW Magazine. There were both straight men and women, although the majority were women. Joey chuckled. Prostitutes mainly used the personals, even though it was illegal in Toronto. He figured their disguises helped keep the police at bay, or that the authorities simply didn't care. They all had secrets hidden in well-written ads.

He had been thinking about restarting his massage services, similar to what he did in Key West. The city's large population made it an ideal location, and he believed its gay community was both thriving and sizable. He intended to offer his services privately at his apartment, with a massage table set up in the living room. He found a medical supply store on Yonge Street and a store called the Body Shop, which sold oils, herbs, incense, and New Age music CDs. Getting supplies wouldn't be an issue. The main thing he needed was more towels and linens, which he could purchase at Holt Renfrew, a nearby store where he bought linens earlier that day. They had a wide selection of bath towels that would be perfect for his needs.

It wasn't that he needed the money; that was certain. He needed something to do with his free time, which was all of it every day. He would be able to meet people, some of whom would become regular clients, and hopefully, if things worked out, a few friends as well.

He hadn't done so yet, but he would have to decorate and prepare the second bathroom for use by his clients. It was strategically located off the hallway, so he would not have to use the master bath off his bedroom. It had a sink, toilet, and a shower stall that would be perfect for them to use after their massage. With his built-in washer and dryer, keeping a supply of fresh towels and linens would not be a problem.

The following morning, Joey executed his plan, starting with a trip to buy towels—he purchased a dozen large, plush, and costly white ones. He concluded that linens were unnecessary since he could cover the massage table with one of the nearly five-foot-long towels. Once that was completed and a load was in the washing machine, he headed to the medical supply store where he bought a folding, portable massage table. He didn't plan on it, but if an outcall arose, he could take it with him. He also stopped by the Body Shop and picked up a dozen bottles of lightly scented almond oil and three CDs containing new age music geared toward relaxation.

Once back in his living room, he set up the table and looked at it. Draping a towel over it, he put one of the CDs in the sound system and turned it on. The music, he decided, was perfect, but still, something was missing. Then an idea came to him. Grabbing his coat, he headed out again. There were two more things he needed to do.

As Shayne crossed the border into Canada, the reality of being back hit him like a slap in the face. Winter was all around him as he drove up Highway 81 toward Hamilton. It was snowing heavily, enough to engage the Jeep's 4-wheel drive. Typically, it would take no more than an hour and a half to reach Toronto from where he was, but with the weather, he figured more like two, if there were no accidents along the way.

He stopped and managed to get through to Claire, who promised to leave the door key under a flowerpot next to the front door of her duplex apartment. It was located in The Beaches on Woodbine Avenue. Shayne had jotted down the address along with the address of the restaurant where she worked, just in case, then drove onward toward Buffalo, NY. That had been an hour ago, and he was feeling anxious as he approached the city. He was unsure how he felt about returning home and what he would find when he got there. He believed he would find his place and settle in as he usually did, with Claire helping him as she always had.

CHAPTER 3
Final Details & A New Kid in Town

Joey stood back and admired his setup, smiling at how everything had turned out. The massage table was complete with one of the new, freshly washed towels covering it, and the new age music filled the room as well as the entire apartment. He had discovered that the condo had a central control panel in the pantry, which was not much different from the Key West house. There were well-hidden speakers in every room. They were broadcasting relaxing music.

The final addition he made was an aquarium placed next to the massage table. He positioned it perpendicular to the wall, creating a partition between the table and the rest of the living room. The placement allowed for viewing the tropical fish from either side of the tank. The bubbles rising from the bottom and the movement of the fish enhanced his effort to create complete relaxation during the massage, hopefully lulling his client into a state of full bliss. The happy ending he provided would be the cherry on top of a luxurious experience. Finally, he invested in a new cell phone, much smaller than the one he had in Key West. This one had a retractable antenna and folded to fit in his pocket. He considered its $4500.00 price tag worth the cost.

The final step involved stopping at the offices of NOW Magazine to place his ad in the personals section. Joey had given it some thought and decided to take an ad from another advertiser and modify the wording for his use. What he assumed was that his competition had headlined his ad with "For Men Only," followed by a pampered massage by Greg. "Let me relax your body as only another man can," and come up with his own: Man 4 Man, followed by a massage by Joey. A complete full-body experience that always has a happy ending.

Satisfied, he paid the $55.00 for the week and left. It would appear in a few days with the new issue. He tried to pre-pay for the month, but they didn't offer it, so he would have to stop by weekly to renew his ad.

Another thing he had yet to decide was how much to charge for his service. To get an idea, he decided to call Greg and pretend to be a potential client. It wouldn't hurt to get a feeling for his competition and how he presented himself.

"Greg speaking, how may I help you?" The deep voice of a man answered Joey's telephone call after only two rings. Greg was prompt if nothing else.

"I am interested in your service. I am visiting on business and need a massage. Can you describe yourself and what your service is?" Joey found himself trying to disguise his voice, then thought it was silly. He had never met Greg, so why bother?

"I'm blonde with blue eyes, and six feet tall with large hands." Greg began his proposition. "I provide a full-body massage using a warm oil that lasts an hour. I charge $65.00."

"Sex?" Joey asked.

"Well, I'm not opposed to having a little fun as long as it's safe," Greg replied. "I discuss that only once you are here, never over the phone."

"So", Joey thought there was sex involved, but how much and what it entailed was still a mystery.

"How big are you?" Joey thought he was pushing his luck.

Greg didn't seem to mind the question at all. "I'm eight inches and semi-cut."

"Semi?"

"I have what you might consider a convertible model." Greg laughed. "The foreskin only partially hides my penis."

Joey laughed, trying to imagine. In doing so, he found himself getting aroused by the man. He needed to hang up. "Let me check my schedule and call you back, ok?"

"Sure, no problem. If I don't answer, leave a message as I am more than likely with a client."

"Thanks," Joey said and hung up.

$65.00 was far less than what he earned in Key West, but Toronto wasn't a resort town, and most people weren't there on vacation. His new clients would likely be men who worked and lived in the Toronto area, seeking the touch of another man. He fully expected married men to come through his door, just like many had back in Florida, curious about what the experience with another man would be like. Joey was more than happy to introduce them to the joys of being with another man, though not always, through sex. The hand job he gave at the end of his treatments was often enough to persuade some men that the experience deserved further exploration: there was no commitment or emotional maneuvering like that required with a woman—just getting off–uncomplicated by feelings or emotions. That's what these men want, Joey thought.

Shayne found Claire's townhouse. She had prepared the guest bedroom for him as well as left out a bottle of wine and a glass in case he wished to have a drink after his long drive.

He considered it, then decided he would wait and familiarize himself with her flat. It was a two-story house with three bedrooms, all of which were located on the second floor. She had had two lesbian roommates, but one moved out of the townhouse to return to University, and she had yet to lease it. Shayne considered himself lucky that she hadn't, as it now was his. He had plenty of money to pay his share of the rent and utilities and could continue to do so for the remainder of the year if he chose to. He decided not to and instead searched for employment as soon as he was settled. He still had to drive the few miles south to see his parents and his sister. There was plenty of time to do both. For now, he wanted to get out into the city to see what might be new and what had stayed the same. He wondered if anything had changed at Komrad's, his go-to nightclub, which he used to patronize.

He pulled the piece of paper he had jotted down where Claire was working and decided to see her and have something to eat. He was hungry, and Italian sounded splendid on an empty stomach. He showered, changed his clothes, and called a cab, because parking on a Friday night would be difficult. He didn't want the hassle of it. Dino's, he read. It must be a new place, because he had never heard of it, having spent the majority of his teens and early twenties haunting its gay establishments. He was only seventeen when he used a fake ID along with his good looks to get into Komrad's, which led to him losing his virginity at an older man's apartment a few blocks away from the disco. From that night on, Komrad's became his place to party and find sex.

Komrads would have to wait for another night, and there would be many. Tonight, he would settle for dinner at the new restaurant and see his old friend, whom he had not seen in a long time. A horn sounded from outside, and a glance at his watch told him it was 7:30 p.m. Smiling, he slid his wallet into his back pocket and skipped out the door.

It was Friday afternoon when Joey's cell phone rang for the first time. Since no one he knew had that number, he assumed it was related to his advertisement. Recognizing Greg's deep voice immediately, he listened as Greg, pretending to be a potential client, asked about **his** services, just as Joey had done when calling Greg. Joey didn't let Greg continue and revealed that they had already spoken a few days earlier. He shared details about his move to Toronto and his previous work in Key West, where he operated a massage business, and now plans to establish one here in Toronto. He had needed information on what the market was like and how much he should charge. Greg had provided him with what he needed to know. Both had a good laugh about the situation and decided to meet for a drink or dinner to share stories. Despite being competitors, they saw no reason not to be friends; the city was big enough for both. They chose Dino's; they both had been there and liked the food. It was Friday, and Dino's didn't accept reservations, and they knew they might need to wait.

Before Joey left for Dino's, his phone rang again, and he answered it. This time, it wasn't Greg; it was a man inquiring about his services. He explained what he did and the cost, sidestepping a question about sex. The man scheduled an appointment for the following evening at 8 pm. Joey gave him his address and told him to use the buzzer in the lobby, and he would send the elevator down since he lived on the penthouse level. There were no hallways or public elevators leading to the 33rd floor of 25 The Esplanade.

Perfect, Joey thought as he hung up. His ad had been in NOW Magazine for less than a day, and he already had an appointment set up. It made him wonder what would happen once the publication was fully distributed throughout the city. It wouldn't take long for him to find out.

Greg was standing outside of Dino's, and Joey recognized him immediately by the way he had described himself. He was a large individual. Not fat, just large in stature. The clothing he was wearing fit him well, not loose or baggy. What they revealed was a typical man in his thirties, who was attractive but not in the same league as Joey, who turned heads wherever he went. Tonight was no different, and there were catcalls from strangers on the street, which Joey loved but ignored.

"It seems that you are quite popular with strangers," Greg said, stepping up and holding out his hand for Joey to shake. "I'm Greg, Greg Scheske, and yes, that is my real name. I don't use an alias for my business."

"Joey. Joey Wilde, and yes, that is my actual name. I didn't pick it; it came with the body." Joey shook Greg's hand, smiling, showing off his perfect teeth. "I get that a lot. Strangers ogling me. I'm sorry about it."

"Why, sorry? I can only wish I were so good-looking to afford such compliments." He replied, opening the door for Joey. "I didn't know I was dining with a rock star tonight. Love the hair."

Joey stepped inside the restaurant. He spied Claire, and she smiled and waved, holding up her finger, motioning for him to wait.

"My favorite new customer!" Claire chirped, referring to Joey, as she skipped up to greet her guests. "Hi, Greg. Long time no see. Where ya been?"

"Here and there. Busy with things."

"I take it you two are together, so table for two?" She asked.

"You got it. "Greg replied.

She gathered up two menus and led them to a secluded table.

The two ordered and sat back, chatting as they waited for their meals.

"So, why the move?" Greg asked, as he took the bottle of wine he ordered, pouring a glass for Joey first, then for himself. "I can't see anyone choosing to live here instead of Key West. It must have been something major that made you move."

"I knew a man who lived here in Toronto. A real estate attorney named David. I was his escort."

"I can certainly see why he chose you." Greg thought for a moment. "I knew a lawyer named David. Yeah, David Shortill. He recently died from AIDS."

Joey couldn't believe how small the world was. "That's him." He replied. "I was in his will."

Greg whistled. "David Shortill was a prominent attorney in Toronto, and I know that he represented a lot of wealthy clients, including businesses. I can only imagine how much he left to you."

Joey said, "Let's just say it was enough for me to retire partially. He also left me his car and a condo at 25 The Esplanade, where I currently live. You should come see it sometime."

Greg whistled. "The Esplanade. I'd love to. I've only been in the building once, to a friend's apartment on the 9th floor. I remember the lobby being spectacular."

"It is. I was surprised by it myself," Joey said, taking a sip of the wine, its bitter-sweet flavor bursting onto his palate and down his throat. It was comforting on a cold evening. "I'm on the 33rd floor, penthouse number 2. I plan on doing the massage out of my living room."

Greg whistled again. "Penthouse, no less. I hear that they have a private elevator. Is that true?"

"A shared elevator. It has a door on either side of it. I use a code to access it, and it drops me off in my living room. The other door opens into PH 1."

"How cool is that. I live in a penthouse as well on Sherbourne Street, but nothing as fancy as what you have. And I rent. I have to buzz my clients in at the front door, and they have to take the elevator to my apartment using the hallway." He laughed. "Imagine having to use a hallway."

Joey knew Greg was teasing him and laughed along. Then, their food arrived, and they started eating. As before, Joey chose the chicken parm, and Greg went with a plate of fettuccini carbonara. The bread was warm and fresh, the food was delicious, the wine was exquisite, and the company was delightful. Both men agreed they should have dinner again soon as they parted ways outside the restaurant. Joey hailed a cab and headed home. He had to prepare for his first client. On the way home, his phone rang again.

"Hey, you!" Claire said happily, wrapping her arms around Shayne's neck, hugging him ferociously. "Any problems?" She asked.

"None at all. I put all of my things in the bedroom you prepared for me, which reminds me that I want to give you money tomorrow. Don't let me forget to do so."

"Forget about that. Tell me about your trip. I have a few minutes."

Shayne provided her with a brief summary of his recent days, excluding some of the more unpleasant moments he had with Jonathan. It would stay his secret, the hidden abuse that he endured.

"I'm starved. Is there a table available?"

"Yeah, two guys just left before you came in. One of them was in here before, and I tell you what, a drop-dead good-looking young man—muscles on muscles and long hair. When I first saw him, I thought he was a rock star and a member of one of those big-hair bands. There are a few of them here in Toronto."

"Sounds like a friend I knew back in Key West. I lost track of him."

"That's awful. Isn't there any way of finding him? Family or something?"

"No. I only know that he was from Maine. He had a lover in Key West, but the relationship went sour, so he left the island. The last I knew of him, he was coming to Toronto to collect an inheritance from a man for whom he had been an escort, but I don't know if he stayed or took the money and ran. If he is here, maybe I will bump into him. We were getting to be very close friends, and I was even hoping for more than that before he got involved with that doctor who screwed him over."

"How terrible," Claire said and looked up. "I have to check on my tables. I'll be back to take your order."

"A Blue and the special of the day. See how easy that was?"

She smiled, scribbled the order onto her bill pad." You got it. Be back soon."

He watched her walk off and thought of Joey and where he could be. Why hadn't he gotten more information from him about his dealings in Toronto? At least something would have given him a clue to track his friend. There were 3.5 million people in the city. Joey could be anywhere.

His beer arrived, followed by his food, which he ate alone at the table.

CHAPTER 4
Komrad's and Uomo

Paul Stenhouse was not your typical male prostitute and made his money not by way of the street but through a tabloid. NOW Magazine offered him the means of attracting men with whom he was paid handsomely for sex. To him, it didn't matter what kind of sex it was. He would cater to the most exotic of fetishes because he found out there were many.

He was also a drug user, his primary choice of narcotic being ecstasy, which he found most useful when he needed to perform sexual acts outside of the norm. His price for an evening of debauchery would range from two hundred dollars up to over a thousand, depending on what was asked of him. Anything involving BDMS was priced at the high end, which a night of getting fucked might fetch a couple of hundred. He was strictly a bottom and was built for it.

He was 135 pounds, and his 5'6" frame was more feminine than masculine. Sometimes this led him to dress up in drag at a client's request, even altering his voice to sound like a young girl. He had a few dresses at home, along with more sexy outfits with garters and nylons that he could wear when needed. He mostly did outcalls and found himself in lavish hotels regularly, but he also extended the use of his bedroom to certain men he saw regularly.

He did take time off for himself and usually spent it at Komrad's, partying like the twenty-year-old that he was and drinking sometimes to the point where the bouncer would ask him to leave and call him a cab. Friday night was an exception, and he was keeping the drinking to a minimum as he swirled and danced on Konrad's massive dance floor.

He wasn't a drop-dead, good-looking guy, but his petite build made him very attractive to some who fancied such. Although he was twenty, Paul appeared to be younger, eighteen or less, to the liking of some men. He used this to his advantage when charging for his services. He was a talented and effective actor when needed.

He was new to the game, having become a high-end hustler only a few months ago. His lover, a man several years older than him, had died of AIDS, which left Paul distraught and led him into deep depression. He clawed his way out of it by discovering that he could not only make money through sex but that it also gave him a sense of belonging and made him feel cared for—something that had been missing since Carl's death. Some of the things he was asked to do were degrading and difficult for him at times, but the rewards far outweighed the lows of his chosen profession. Most of his clients treated him with respect and dignity. As he brought new men into his circle, he was gradually filtering out the undesirables. He was getting close to having regular sex and getting paid handsomely.

This Friday night, he was off with nothing pending, so he decided to go to Komrad's for some fun. It was there that he saw Shayne.

Joey's buzzer went off five minutes before the scheduled appointment, and he took a moment to look at a monitor on the kitchen bar to see who it was. Another perk of the penthouse was the closed-circuit security system, which allowed him to screen his guests before sending the elevator to fetch them.

On the monitor was a young, chubby man, who Joey guessed was in his twenties. Not his typical client by any stretch of the imagination, as he was used to older men. He pressed a button next to the screen, and a green light flashed, indicating to Joey that the elevator was descending. He waited and watched until he saw the man step into the elevator, then waited for his arrival.

He prepared everything well in advance of his first customer's-arrival. The new age music played softly in the background; the table was set with a warm, fresh towel, and his oil was heated and ready in the microwave. The man's name was Joe, and he wondered if he might have gone by the name Joey. Joey was his given name, not Joe or Joseph, and he was glad that his parent had named him such. He didn't like formal names, and the name Joe did not suit him.

Unlike most elevators, it did not signal its arrival with a ding. Not in the apartment, which would have been an annoyance. Down in the lobby, it was fine, however. The door slid open, and Joe stepped out into the living room. He took one look at Joey, and Joey could tell that he was nervous. It was likely his first time receiving a massage. An erotic one at that, so Joey did his best to comfort and calm him.

"Hi and welcome," Joey said in a calm, neutral voice. "I hope you didn't have any trouble finding the place."

"Not at all," Joe said meekly. "I live on the 7th floor. A one-bedroom that I rent. I was surprised when you told me you were in the same building in the penthouse. Very cool."

"It is," Joey replied and realized that Joe was not wearing a winter coat. He didn't need to, because all he had to do was take the elevator to the lobby and switch elevators. "Come in, I'm set up in the living room."

Joe was impressed by what he saw. The living room was large, but Joey had set up a niche for his massage. He was impressed by his use of the professional table and told him so. He had gone to others who rubbed him down on an uncomfortable bed that was too soft.

"So, it wasn't this guy's first time after all." Joey thought of retrieving the oil.

Joe seemed to enjoy the ambient music as well.

Joey handed him a towel and asked Joe to get undressed and lie face down on the table, his nose in the hole where the head would be. The well-positioned padded hole allowed for the patient to lie perfectly flat without discomfort.

"I'll be back in just a moment, so please get ready," Joey said, then left to allow Joe the privacy to undress.

Upon his return, Joey adjusted the music volume and dimmed the lights, highlighting the city lights visible from his condo. The lights of the aquarium were soft and inviting, its aerator humming--barely audible–with the new age music enhancing the ambiance. Joe was quickly lulled into the serenity of the moment.

Joe was on the table, the towel Joey had given him draped across his ass, his clothing neatly folded on the chair next to the aquarium. Joey didn't say a word, and he poured oil onto the palm of his hands, rubbing them together before beginning to massage and caress the muscles on Joe's neck and shoulders. Joe responded by letting out a moan.

Halfway through the massage, he whispered into Joe's ear to please roll over, and as he did so, he exposed a six-inch-long, stiff cock that stood straight up. Joe didn't seem embarrassed or bothered by it and lay waiting for Joey to begin once again.

Joey started at the soles of Joe's feet and worked slowly up his body, kneading and rubbing his flesh with swirling motions The smile on Joe's face was evidence of the pleasure that Joey was giving him. He avoided Joe's erection altogether and continued up, completing the massage, working the scalp, which he had found most men enjoyed immensely. He then returned to Joe's chest and began to use long, sensual movements downward.

Joey always did his work in the nude and found that it more than enhanced what he was doing to a body that was under his expert touch. As he leaned over Joe's head to run his hand over his stomach, it afforded Joe an excellent view of Joey cock and balls as they hung inches from Joe's face.

Joey moved to Joe's side and prepared to give Joe the happy ending he had paid for. Working painfully slow, he took Joe's erect cock in his oiled hand and began to stroke like the massage he had just given, working from his tight balls, up the shaft, then using the palm of his hand to massage the head, returning to repeat the process. It took all of three times and less than a minute for Joe to moan loudly and climax, shooting a stream of cum onto his stomach and covering Joey's hands.

Joey lingered for a few moments longer before removing his hands completely from Joe's softened penis. Joe took a deep breath and opened his eyes.

"Wow." He managed to say and sat up. "That was the best massage I have ever had, Joey. You are very talented."

"Thanks, Joey said, using a fresh towel to wipe Joe's stomach. "I have a shower in the hall if you would like to use it."

Joe shook his head. "Remember, I live here, or down on the 7th floor. I can use this towel to wipe some of this oil off, so I won't get too much on my clothes."

"Sure. Take your time." Joey said and went to the sink to wash his hands.

Ten minutes later, Joe had already made another appointment for the following week, handed Joey the $65.00, and stepped into the waiting elevator.

Joey stuffed the money into a jar that he kept in the kitchen cupboard and wondered how long it would take him to fill it. He closed the door, placed the dirty laundry into the washing machine, and went to take a shower. Everything had gone better than he had hoped, and he would continue the same process with his next customer.

Two weeks had passed, and Monday morning was marked by the absence of the foul weather that had been plaguing the city for nearly a week, replaced with sunshine and mild temperatures that promised to be in the low fifties. Joey had seen two issues of NOW Magazine advertising his services, and so far, the results had been promising. He had picked up two more regular clients, bringing the total to three. He massaged another three, but they had not called back for another appointment. After dressing, he decided to head down to the garage and check on his cars. Soon, he hoped he could take them out onto the open road.

Shayne rose early; he had an interview at a modeling agency. Trying the very competitive field may pay off this time. This time, he hoped it was not for some department store to market their shorts; he hoped for something more glamorous and to make a name for himself. Something like expensive designer suits or even men's cologne would do fine. He also hoped that if he got the gig, it would pay commensurate with his looks and what the market dictated. Past experiences with money had been pitiful. He decided before going that if the offer were not what he wanted, he would decline it. He had his principles and wasn't a kid anymore.

As it turned out, the modeling agency that he was going to was one of the most prestigious in all of Canada. Shayne had spent a portion of the previous week at a photographer's building the portfolio that he now held in his hands. The one thing missing was past work, other than the department store. So, he was presenting himself as a potential newcomer. He didn't even have an agent to represent him. Shayne knew his chances were slim, and the entire effort was no more than a shot in the dark. Still, he owed it to himself to try.

As he sat in the agency's waiting room, the first thing he noticed was that he was the only one there. Maybe other models had been there and left. It puzzled him.

He stood and walked to a magazine stand near the entrance and picked up the new issue of NOW Magazine, sat down, and leafed through it. Apart from a few articles of varied interest, most of it was filled with ads. He turned to the personals and skimmed through them, finding nothing of interest. Men seeking men were probably old queens desperate for a date or a spur-of-the-moment sexual encounter. Then he spotted a small ad at the bottom of the page where the personal section ended and professional services began. He read it and dropped his portfolio onto the floor. "Man 4 Man: Massage by Joey, A complete full-body experience that always has a happy ending."

Shayne reread it and thought that it couldn't be. Not his Joey, but the similarities were too much to dismiss. The ad sounded like Joey Wilde had written it, and he knew no one else who used the term "happy ending" to refer to a hand job. There was a number at the end of the ad, and Shayne was anxious to call it as soon as he had the chance.

"Shayne?" A man asked from an open door.

"Here," Shayne said, folding the magazine and tucking it into the inner pocket of his jacket. He stood up and shook the man's outstretched hand.

"My name is Douglas Bouchard," He said, all the while looking Shayne up and down. "Interesting he said. Come this way, please."

He led Shayne down a hall that had small offices on either side of it, men and women busy at desks. Douglas opened a door at the very end and walked inside, motioning Shayne to follow. Once inside, he motioned for Shayne to sit down in front of a large ornate desk, joining him on the other side of it, and plopping down in an expensive-looking leather chair.

"So, you're a model," Douglas said matter-of-factly.

"Yes," Shayne answered, placing his portfolio onto the desk.

Douglas picked it up and flipped through it, stopping only for a moment to look at Shayne's partially nude body, the eyebrow lifting over one eye. "Very interesting. Do you have an agent?"

Shayne shook his head no. "Not yet."

Douglas looked at Shayne, then opened his desk drawer and took out a business card. "Call this one. She is the best in the business." He said, handing it to Shayne.

Shayne remained silent, briefly reading the card as the man examined his photos. After a few minutes, Douglas closed the album, set it down on the desk, leaned back, and looked directly at Shayne. "I'm not necessarily seeking an experienced model, and I don't place much importance on portfolios, except to review the subject I am considering for the job. Every project is different, so a model who excels in one shoot might struggle in another. Modeling is a highly personal experience for both the model, the photographer, and the intended audience. For instance, clothing models aim to make potential buyers imagine themselves in the clothes, hoping to make a sale. This is one of the simplest types of modeling. The model I need will be asked to do more, as the product's success depends on his appearance and how he presents it. This gig is primarily for television, although it will also involve print materials. It will cover all of North America and parts of Europe, making it a great opportunity for the right person. I wonder, Shayne, are you the man I am looking for?"

Shayne began to answer, but Douglas motioned him not to and stood to look out over the city. "The one thing I like about you, Shayne, is your looks, especially the scar on your face. Some would consider it a deal breaker, but I find it extremely sexy, and I believe others will as well. Let me tell you about the gig." He said and sat back down.

Shayne was feeling more optimistic. He sat in the office for nearly thirty minutes, listening to Douglas explain the job's details. It involved a new, luxurious Versace men's cologne called Uomo, which was high-end and exclusive, requiring a man who could personalize it and promote it to others. The name Uomo, meaning "man" in Italian, indicated the target image: a masculine, rugged-looking man with a soft-spoken demeanor, necessary for the commercial's concluding speech. The model needed a well-defined physique that makeup artists could shape into a "warrior" appearance. Shayne was chosen to embody the ideal man envisioned by the client—someone who would appeal to both women and men. The client's main goal was sales, regardless of who purchased the cologne. The marketing approach aimed at heterosexual men, however, featured the model alongside a stunning woman who would appear to be entirely taken by her man, mainly due to the cologne. After considering this further, Douglas reached out to Shayne again, this time to congratulate him—he had been selected to represent Versace's new men's cologne line, Uomo.

"Any questions?" Douglas asked.

Shayne had a million swirling in his head, but shook his head no.

"Good. The shoot is tentatively scheduled for this Spring as the cologne will be released in the fall, so everything needs to be wrapped up by then. With me so far?"

"Yes."

"Good, the shoot will last ten days and will be here in Toronto in our studios upstairs in this building. Your compensation will be 6000.00 Canadian dollars per day for the duration of the shoot. Still, a photograph is included in that, meaning you don't get paid more for what is printed in magazines or other similar media. Fair enough?"

"Very fair," Sayne replied, not quite believing what he was being told, but continued to listen to Douglas as he continued.

Very well, I will need you to return to this office no later than Friday and no earlier than Wednesday to sign the contract and pick up your retainer, which is 20% of one day's work, or $1200.00. The contract is binding. I don't want my new discovery to wander off.

"There is no chance of that happening," Shayne reassured him. "Oh, I just returned to Toronto not long ago, and I am currently staying with a friend. I can give you her number. She has an answering machine so you can leave a message if I am not home and needed."

"If I were you, I would invest in one of the new cell phones that are available. I have a feeling you are going to need it. They are costly, ranging from several thousand dollars. Can you afford one?"

Shayne said that he could and would look into it as soon as he had the time. He would also be back on Wednesday before noon to sign the contract."

With their business wrapped up, Douglas showed Shayne out. "Call that agent." Douglas reminded him and disappeared back into the offices. He took the elevator to the ground floor and stepped out into the sunshine, still trying to wrap his mind around what had just happened. The first thing he wanted to do was to tell Claire, and she was just a few blocks away, working the day shift at Dino's. Whistling happily, he decided to walk.

CHAPTER 5
The Horseshoe

Joey started the Camero first, listening to it roar to life, then fall back into a gentle purr. The eight-cylinder motor had reached its break-in mileage and surpassed it with its trip from Miami to Toronto, a distance of 1,500 miles recommended by Chevrolet. He turned it off, stuffed the key into his pocket, and then uncovered the Ferrari. It was a Testarossa, and beautiful, with its quality far surpassing that of the Camaro, which sat next to it. He opened the door and sat in the driver's seat. The interior was of soft Italian leather that seemed to hug his body, drawing him into the luxury. The entire makeup was a work of art.

He turned the key, and the 12-cylinder sounded especially loud inside the underground garage, but soon quieted to a gentle purr. Joey turned on the radio, but there was only static. Because he was underground, the concrete blocked any signal. It did have a tape deck, however, and he had a large selection of tapes to choose from in the apartment. He looked at himself in the rearview mirror, then turned off the car. He couldn't wait to take it out and drive it. The weather had to improve for that to happen.

He climbed out and covered both cars, then went back to his apartment. He had a new appointment coming soon.

Claire shrieked and threw herself into the arms of Shayne. "I can't believe that you got it! And it's a TV commercial too. This is big time, Shayne."

"Well, I haven't even signed the contract yet." Shayne cautioned, but inside, he was just as excited for himself as Claire was. "The new cologne is called Uomo, which I think means "man" in Italian."

"Versace is Italian, and I think he's gay. I read somewhere that he is considering a move to the United States, possibly to Florida.

"Must be nice to be rich, eh?"

"Since when did you get your Canadian accent back?" Claire asked, giggling.

"I didn't. That was a cough." He said, smiling.

"Right. Look, I have to get ready for the noon-time rush. I'm off at 3 pm today. Wanna celebrate and have a drink? Maybe at The Horseshoe? They have a great special from 3 pm to 7 pm, two for one wells and beers."

"That sounds great! It will give me time to go shopping for a cell phone. Douglas, er, the guy who hired me, said I should get one as I would need it. It seems that I need an agent as well."

"Big time, Shayne. Now, let me go. Come get me at 3 pm, ok?"

"You got it, Kitten." He said and watched her walk off.

"Kitten." He thought. He hadn't called Claire that in years. He had been calling her that nickname ever since he visited her bedroom when they were pre-teenagers. She had a massive collection of stuffed cats all around her room and seemed obsessed with them. Thus, he started calling her "Kitten," and the name stuck. He wondered why he had forgotten it, perhaps due to his being away in Key West?

He needed to find a store that sold cell phones, but he had no idea where to start looking. Radio Shack came to mind, so he decided to start there. He remembered there was one in the mall on Yonge Street, and he could take a cab there.

As he sat in the front of the taxi, he ran through what had just happened in his mind again. This could be a significant breakthrough for him if things work out. Television was a huge media outlet for a young model like himself, and what other opportunities might arise from this first chance? "Joey would be proud and happy for me," he thought.

Joey.

Shayne could have kicked himself in the ass if he had not been sitting down. He had forgotten entirely about the advert in NOW Magazine. Joey could be nearby and just a phone call away. As soon as he finished at Radio Shack, he would find a telephone and call the number. Hell, if he bought the phone, he would use it. His stomach was suddenly tying itself into nervous knots. He could only hope that the man advertising was *his* Joey.

The taxi stopped at the curb, and Shayne got out, handing the driver a folded bill. The driver thanked Shayne and then sped off. He looked at the tall building ahead, rising about fifty stories into the sky. The mall was on the first and second floors. He headed inside.

Joey's new client was a referral from Joe, who lived downstairs on the 7th floor of his building. He knew because the man whose name is James told him so when he called and made the appointment. The only other thing he knew about the man was that he was an executive at the bank where Joe worked and was not openly gay. Joey would see for himself within the hour.

"Here it is!" The salesman said proudly, handing Shayne something that resembled a brick. "The Nokia Cityman 900. The very latest in affordable cell phone technology."

Shayne turned it over in his hands. It was slimmer than others he had seen in restaurants, but it was heavy. "Anything lighter?" He asked.

"That is the lightest there is, but they are always working on something new and improved." The salesman was unaware of a newer, smaller model that a competitor had recently released. As far as he knew, the Nokia was the latest.

Shayne didn't have time for a company to introduce a new model. He was going to have to take what he could get. "How much?"

"$3995.00 and that includes a six-month warranty, and we activate it for you and give you a telephone number, all included in the price."

Shayne whistled. It was expensive. Not that he couldn't afford it, as he had a tidy sum saved up from his time with Jonathan, and the new gig was going to bring in 60K. "Does it have an answering service?"

"Unfortunately, no."

This new cell phone thing wasn't living up to the hype, but still, he had to consider not having it, especially when working as a model. "What else do I need to know about it?" Shayne asked, taking another look at the phone.

"This new model has an hour of talk time compared to its predecessor, which then has to be charged." The salesman said, pointing to the charging port. Just plug it into any available wall socket. There is a $100 per month fee, and calls are billed at 50 cents per minute, whether you make or receive them."

Shayne would have to keep his calls short, or it would cost him a fortune. He thought for a few more minutes, the salesman patiently waiting.

"Ok, I'll take it," Shayne said. "Do you take a credit card? I don't normally walk around with that much cash."

"Well, of course. Mastercard, Visa, or American Express. We take them all."

Shayne dug out his wallet, produced his Toronto Dominion Visa card, and handed it to him.

"Let me get a new one, and they will set it up for you in the back. It should take approximately an hour to complete everything. Would you like to wait or come back for it?"

"I'll go grab a bite to eat and then come back," Shayne said. "He would look for a payphone and call the number in the advert.

"Let me ring this up and run your card. I won't be but a minute."

Shayne watched him start the process and waited.

Joey's client was running late but had called to say that he would be there at 1:30 pm instead of 1 pm. He was okay with it because he had no other appointments and nothing else planned. He made himself a Pearl Harbor at the bar in the dining area and sat down on the couch to wait. He picked up NOW Magazine and flipped to his advertisement. He was considering making a slight change. He would give it some thought.

His doorbell rang precisely at 1:30 pm, prompting Joey to check the CCTV. Down in the lobby, a man in his forties dressed in a suit stood with his hands behind his back. He pressed the button to send the elevator, then watched as the man. Joey moved to the microwave to restart it for heating the oil, waiting for the elevator to arrive. Moments later, the door slid open, and his client stepped into the living room. Joey greeted him, and the routine commenced, beginning with Joey turning off his cell phone.

Shayne found a bank of six vacant payphones near the restroom. He fished in his pocket and pulled out a quarter, and with the magazine in hand, he dialed the number. It began to ring, then rang some more before it stopped with a click. He tried one more time with the same result. Maybe Joey was busy? He would try again later. He did a little window shopping and headed back to Radio Shack. They had just finished setting up his new phone, and after a quick tutorial on how to use it, along with signing the contracts with Bell for service, he left the store.

Once on the street, he turned it on and confirmed that it worked and that he had a service connection. What he didn't have was much talk time, as the battery showed it was low. He turned it off, tucked it into his pocket, which was a tight fit, and looked for a cab to hail. It was nearing 2 pm, and he had to meet Claire in an hour. He would go back to Dino's and wait for her, maybe have a beer. As he sat in the back of the cab, he couldn't help but think of Joey and hope.

Joey had finished the massage, and his customer was raving about how good it was and how it was a bargain at $65.00 an hour. Joey had noticed the wedding ring on the man's finger during the rub down, and the man had noticed that Joey had seen it.

"Yeah. I'm married to a woman." He said apologetically, as if Joey cared.

"That's cool," Joey said.

"Well, seeing a masseur wouldn't exactly look good for a man in my position, you understand. I want to keep this just between the two of us."

"I pride myself on preserving the confidentiality of all of my clients," Joey said, repeating what he had said to countless other clients.

"That's good. Well, it will be our little secret."

He also inquired about getting a two-hour treatment. Joey had the feeling that he was fishing to see if Joey would provide sexual services, so he told him not as a rule, but he would think about it. Joey took his money, jotted down when he would like to come next, and then showed the man out.

"I'll see you next week," Joey said as the elevator door slid closed. It seemed that he added another regular to his clientele.

Joey received $80.00. He had been given a tip. Joey stuffed the money into the jar in the cupboard and took a shower.

Claire was able to leave work a little early, and she was waiting for him when he arrived. He skipped the beer at Dino's and the two of them walked the block and a half to the Horseshoe.

Steam wafted around Joey as he rinsed off the remaining oil, his mind replaying the day's encounter. The distant noises of the city seeped in through the bathroom window—traffic sounds and distant horns--- giving him the feeling of anonymity. After drying off and dressing swiftly, he moved to the kitchen, where the smell of stale coffee lingered. He poured himself a black, bitter cup while listening to the ticking clock and the soft hum of the fridge.

A glance at his phone reminded him to turn it on so he wouldn't miss a potential client call. He settled at the kitchen bar, flipping through his calendar, contemplating the meaning of secrets—those belonging to him, his clients', and the ones quietly hidden in conversations or aftercare exchanges. He pondered how many of his regulars, like the man with the wedding ring, were caught between desire and obligation, and how many new faces might appear as news of his services spread.

Outside, sunlight slanted across the city's edges, creating long shadows on the sidewalk. Joey finished his coffee, grabbed his wallet, and waited for the elevator. He stepped into the afternoon, feeling that the next chapter—whatever it might be—was close, just around the corner, another adventure ready to unfold. He chose to head up Church Street to Wellesley and explore a bit more, perhaps check out a new bar that might serve a bite to eat; he wasn't in the mood for Dino's again. It was still early, so he decided to walk the dozen or so city blocks. He hadn't been working out and felt the need for exercise.

He had walked a few blocks, taking in the various businesses along the way. There were also plenty of people hustling along the sidewalk, most seeming to be in a hurry to get somewhere. Joey was glad to be free to take his time and enjoy the city's sights and sounds.

Forty-five minutes later, he reached the intersection of Wellesley and Church, contemplating his next move. He made his decision swiftly, crossed the street, and turned left. As he walked, he noticed more stores similar to those on Church Street near his building, but this area had an openly gay vibe, with shops displaying rainbow flags and other LGBT-friendly items in their storefronts.

After another couple of blocks, he came across a bar with a menu written out on a chalkboard easel, displayed on the sidewalk. There were two tables set near the entrance, the bar taking advantage of the warmer weather. Both were empty. A sign hung over one of them: The Horseshoe Café and Tavern. It was precisely what Joey was hoping to find. He opened the door and stepped inside.

The bar was larger than it looked from the outside. Although not wide, it extended a good distance toward the back of the building. A long counter ran along the left wall, with tables set up in the center and to the right.

A sign that sat on another easel read "Please seat yourself," so Joey did, choosing a booth near the end of the bar. After a few minutes, a young, flamboyant man appeared and took his order: a Caesar salad and a glass of Pinot Grigio wine before skipping off to the bar. Joey watched as the waiter talked to the bartender, another young man who kept glancing in Joey's direction. Joey shook his head, stood up, and went to find the restroom.

Shayne and Claire talked the entire way to the Horseshoe, and he filled her in on all the details of his new modeling job. She had been glued to his every word and was ecstatic about his good fortune. Once inside the bar, they decided to sit outside, and Shayne pulled out a chair for Claire to sit on.

"Thanks!" She said and opened a menu that was pinned between the umbrella shaft and the salt and pepper shakers. "I'm starved. I didn't eat at Dino's and didn't have breakfast this morning. I can go for the burger. The Horseshoe makes a great one."

"That sounds fantastic," Shayne replied, taking his phone out of his pocket and turning it on.

"That thing looks heavy." She commented.

"It is. You might think I'm crazy, but I came across this ad in NOW Magazine."

"And?"

"Remember the guy I mentioned? The one that I met in Key West? His name is Joey and he did massages in Key West. Look here." Shayne took the magazine from his other pocket, opened it to the classifieds, and pointed to Joey's advert. "This guy sounds like him."

"How come he is in Toronto?"

He knew this man from here. He was a paid companion for David, then he died. Joey inherited some money. I don't know how much, and it doesn't matter. I know that he left Key West and would have come here. I think this might be him.

"How cool would that be?"

"I miss him a lot, Claire. We almost became an item, but, well, it didn't happen. Shit got in the way."

"So, call the number, dummy!"

Shayne looked at the phone and back at Claire. "Ok, here goes nothing."

"More like everything if it's him."

Joey had just returned from the restroom when his phone rang. He picked it up and answered it.

"This is Joey. How can I help you?" He said cheerfully.

Shayne nearly dropped his phone. He recognized the voice instantly. It was Joey. "It's him." Joey mouthed the words to Claire, who clapped her hands quietly.

"Joey, this is Shayne."

Joey dropped his phone onto his lap.

CHAPTER 6
A Date with Joey

The two didn't talk long as Shayne's phone was nearly dead, but they managed to set up a meeting for the following day. Joey invited him to dinner. Shayne suggested The Old Spaghetti Factory, which was conveniently located directly across from 25 The Esplanade. Joey saw the restaurant but hadn't gone there yet. With little else being said in the short time they had spoken, Joey was left feeling nervous and excited about seeing Shayne again. He didn't say a final goodbye and felt guilty about it. He hoped that Shayne was not disappointed in Joey for his sudden departure. He wasn't even sure if Shayne knew about everything that transpired between him and JJ. Joey would fill him in over dinner.

Joey finished his meal and dropped the money to pay for it on top of the check the waiter had left on his table. He put the phone back in his pocket, stood, slipped his leather jacket on, and walked out the door.

"Hey, you!" Claire said happily as Joey walked out the door. "It's my favorite new customer. Shayne was sitting with his back to the door and didn't turn to see who she was referring to, as he was busy with his dying cell phone.

"Hey, there," Joey said. "How's it going?"

Shayne quickly turned around, and both men locked eyes. Joey pointed inside, then at Shayne with a confused look. They had just spoken on the phone a few seconds ago, and now here was Shayne in all his handsome glory. They had been sitting no more than ten feet apart, separated only by a wall.

Shayne flew out of his chair and bear hugged Joey, tears welling up in his eyes. "I didn't think I would ever see you again." He said, releasing Joey.

"Aw, you can never get rid of me. It's great to see you, Shayne."

"So," Claire said, pointing to Joey and looking at Shayne. "This is *your* Joey?"

Joey smiled at her use of words. "That's me."

"I can't believe that you were sitting inside all this time," Shayne said. "We could have had lunch together. At least sit down and have a drink while we eat, please?"

"We have a lot to talk about."

"We do, but let's save it for dinner tomorrow, at least some things. We don't want to bore Claire."

"Bore me? Not a chance. I love soap operas! I still can't believe that I met Joey before you found him here!"

"It's weird, and you're not going to get a soap opera from this queen." Shayne kidded.

"You're no fun."

"Go on, Shayne, regale her with our adventures and exploits in Key West." Joey's smile turned into an evil grin as he played along.

'Maybe later."

"Well, I can't stay anyway. I have an appointment, and I don't want to be late. It's a new client."

"How's biz?" Shayne asked as Joey stood up.

"So far, so good. Talk tomorrow, ok?"

"7 pm at the Spaghetti Factory."

"Got it. It was great to see you again, Claire. I guess we are destined to become friends."

Claire smiled broadly. "Seems that way!"

Claire and Shayne watched as Joey walked to the street, hailed a cab, and climbed in the back. The car sped off.

"Can you believe it?" Shayne was still in shock. "What a day this has been."

"Yep. A new job and you got your boyfriend back."

"He's not my boyfriend yet," Shayne said and showed her his crossed fingers. He would be, though, if no one else had come along and beaten him to it. He didn't intend to let Joey slip away a *second* time.

Clark Peterson kissed his wife on the cheek before heading out the door. The CEO of Darlington Enterprises, a Fortune 500 company, was constantly on the go and busy with the many tasks associated with his position. He had come home for lunch and changed out of his suit and tie into something more comfortable. He told her that he had to return to the office for a telephone meeting with a client in Asia, and since everyone would be gone for the evening, he could forgo wearing a suit for the call. As usual, the excuse worked, and she bought it hook, line, and sinker. Usually, when he made such an excuse, he was in truth heading to The Barracks, a gay bathhouse over on Church Street in the gay area of the city. Clark didn't do much there as he feared the AIDS epidemic, which scared him. He would usually hit the "closets" and give some man a blow job through the glory hole while he masturbated. Lately, he had been growing concerned that he might be recognized, so he decided to avoid going for the time being. Instead, he had picked up a NOW Magazine and, in its classifieds, found an ad that was written: Man 4 Man: Massage by Joey. It was the happy ending that caught his eye, and he had called that very day to inquire about the services Joey offered. After speaking with him at length, he had booked an appointment for that same evening. By the way Joey described himself, Clark believed that he was in for a memorable evening.

Clark's wife hadn't minded at all and suspected that he had been seeing other women. She didn't realize that he was seeing men. She had her man for the evening, and he was waiting for her in Mississauga. At $500 for the night, she could manage it, and she needed the attention along with the sex. Her husband was terrible in the bedroom and barely touched her when he was home. Both of them kept their secret sins well hidden.

"Another married man." Joey thought after he finished giving Clark what he was touting as the best massage he had ever had. Joey was far better-looking than the men he met at the bathhouse. The younger men who hung out at the baths mainly were prostitutes charging much more than they were worth, even if it did include various types of sexual acts. Joey's hand job at the end of the massage was an unbelievable experience, all for $65.00. And it was completely private as well. Clark had found a new way to release his stress and tension, and promptly arranged to see Joey twice a week, before giving him a crisp new $100.00 bill. Joey thanked him and flexed his pecs for effect, then slipped his shorts back on, covering his semi-erect cock. It was always a good thing to tease a little and leave them wanting more. Clark had gone with a smile on his face a mile wide.

Joey decided to call it a night and stuffed the oil-stained towels into the washing machine before jumping in the shower. As he lathered up, he thought that his business was doing exceptionally well, and he believed he might have more regulars now than at the height of his time in Key West. He needed to call Greg at some point, as they hadn't talked in a few weeks. He wondered how his business was doing. His ad was always in NOW Magazine, so he must still be doing business. He'd give him a ring after he finished showering.

Chet Stevenson sat in the sauna of The Barracks, sweat pouring off his overweight body, soaking the towel that barely fit around his waist.

The thirty-three-year-old gay lawyer's only opportunity for sex seemed to be at one of the numerous bathhouses that were in and around Church and Wellesley. At the Barracks, he was successful most often. Some men preferred heavier men, especially those who were physically large, referring to them as "bears." Those who sought out people such as Chet were called cubs, an apt name Chet had chosen after hearing it.

Chet considered himself versatile when it came to sex, meaning he was both a bottom and a top. Most large men, at least he believed, were tops, meaning they were the aggressors compared to their smaller subservient counterparts. Still, he enjoyed what he *could* get, sometimes paying for the sex.

That was the case for the young man sitting beside him, named Paul. He had seen him at the baths before, but this was the first chance to talk to him. Upon conversation, he discovered Paul was a hustler and was also highly intoxicated. The young man had taken a drug. Paul had said that for $20.00, he would take Chet to his private room there in The Barracks and that he could do whatever he liked. Chet agreed and soon found himself lying on his back, Paul riding up and down his five-inch, stiff cock, Paul's seven-incher bouncing up and down as he rode.

Paul didn't usually come to the baths, as he had plenty of regular clients who paid him well for his services. But, once in a while, he just wanted to be a plain hustler and have sex for fun, as he had done so a few weeks ago, giving that hunky guy a blow job in the back room. Sean was his name, or something like that. He couldn't remember, as there were so many.

Chet came and put his towel back on and handed Paul the twenty he had in a plastic bag attached to his wrist by a rubber band. He walked to his locker and got dressed, having accomplished his sexual goals. He still had to return to the law offices, where he was a founding partner, and hoped no one would see him as he left The Barracks. He didn't need his dirty little secret to get out and cost him his reputation and position. He looked around cautiously, then disappeared into the crowd that filled the sidewalk.

"I'm fairly busy as well," Greg said to Joey. "I work nearly every day of the week, not many hours, mind you, but still, it leaves little time to do anything that does take time. I want to take a drive up north, for instance, but I would need to take a day or two off for that."

"Why work so much?" JJ asked.

"Pay the rent, my friend. "I tend to work more in the earlier parts of the month, and when I make that amount, then I can relax. What I make from then on is strictly mine. I do ok."

"It sounds like it." Joey reached over to his table and picked up a piece of fruit from a bowl, then bit into it, the sweetness of the golden delicious apple spreading throughout his mouth. He quickly chewed it and swallowed. "Sorry about that. I was hungry and bit into an apple."

Greg laughed. "No worries."

Joey could hear a buzzer go off on the other end of the line.

"Oops, there is Dennis, a regular coming for his treatment. He's not much to look at but has a ten-inch dick."

"Go get 'em, tiger," Joey said and hung up.

It was going on 7 pm and was too early to go to bed, so Joey decided to get dressed and head across the street for a nightcap. There were two bars within the same building, both of which he presumed to be heterosexual; if they served cold beer, then who was to care? Not him.

He dressed in his jeans with a white T-shirt, black biker boots, and threw on his leather jacket. He brushed out his long hair, arranging it around his face, then headed for the elevator.

Brandy's, Joey discovered, was a very popular bar with a dance floor catering to what seemed to him to be guys and girls his age. There wasn't an older person in sight as he looked around. A bar ran from right to left and was being tended by two attractive young girls, both blonde, wearing thigh-length skirts with white T-shirts having "Brandy" written across their breasts. One of the girls noticed Joey as he entered the bar and smiled at him at the same time, elbowing the other girl in her side. She turned and, seeing Joey, smiled as well. Joey smiled back and walked to the bar and sat down on one of the stools.

"Hi," Joey said, removing his jacket and draping it on the back of the stool.

"Well, hello." The girl with the longer hair of the two asked. "Where have you been hiding all my life??"

Joey laughed. "Nowhere. I live across the street."

"Which building? I haven't seen you in here before."

"That's because this is my first time in here. I'm in the 25 building."

She whistled. "The expensive one. Must be nice."

"It's cool," He said. "Can I get a beer?"

"What flavor?"

"How about a Labatt?"

"One Blue coming up." She said and moved down the bar to get it.

Joey paid for the beer and then took a walk around to inspect the place. The dance floor wasn't large, certainly not compared to The Copa back in Key West. Three couples were already dancing to a tune by Madonna.

He finished his beer, used the restroom, and decided it was time to leave. Brandys was a convenient place to grab a beer from time to time. Before crossing the street, he stopped at the spot where he was supposed to meet Shayne the next night. Peering through the windows, he saw that it was a family-oriented establishment, with many people inside. He could see the large cooking vats used to boil the pasta. He couldn't wait to be able to sit with Shayne and talk. Other than the brief encounter outside of The Horseshoe, they hadn't spoken for a long time.

Shayne was right where he said he would be when Joey crossed the street to meet him, in front of the restaurant. Joey walked up and hugged him, having to hold back from giving him a passionate kiss. Toronto was not Key West. Instead, he did as the French and kissed him on each cheek.

"You know, that is not going to cut it," Shayne said, smiling. "But it will have to do for now. Damn, it is so good to see you."

"I feel the same. Shall we go in? I'm starved."

A waitress sat them at a table for two tucked away in a corner. Joey looked over the menu, amazed at how many ways pasta could be prepared and served. There were enough variations that it would take a year to try them all. He settled on a simple spaghetti with meatballs, as did Shayne.

"So, tell me," Shayne began, "why did you leave Key West so suddenly without so much as an I'll see you later?"

Joey had known that question was coming and had partially prepared his answer for it, although he knew it was weak. "I was heartbroken with JJ and just wanted to get far away from him." He said, pouring a glass of the wine that he had ordered, first for Shayne, then for himself.

"Fucking lame, Joey, and you know it. You knew how much I cared for you. Maybe I could have comforted you, but you didn't give me a chance."

Joey nodded and took a drink. "I know that, Shayne. I was an asshole for not seeking you out. But, I think that now, if I had done so, I might have interfered with your plans, such as trying to convince you to come with me to Toronto. At that time, you had your life in order; I would have only been a distraction to those plans."

"Better, but I am still not completely buying it." Shayne took a sip of the wine and frowned: "Screw it, what's done is done. We are here now, no more JJ or Jefferson, the two of us talking like we used to do."

"I am happy that you forgive me," Joey said with a weak smile.

"I didn't say that I did forgive you, but I do. So, you came to Toronto to claim your inheritance from David's estate?"

"Yes, and I decided to stay, although I knew I would be alone here until I could make new friends. Your call was unexpected."

"The ad was the key," Shayne said, taking another sip of his wine. "So, how much did he leave you?"

Joey felt almost embarrassed to say, but went ahead with it. "4.5 million in cash, a house, the condo across the street, his Mercedes-Benz, and a Ferrari." Joey looked up to see Shayne's reaction.

"A Ferrari?" Shayne was not surprised; he was shocked. "Didn't he have any family?"

"No," Joey answered and changed the subject. "How about you, Shayne? Why are you back in Toronto?"

Shayne spilled his guts with everything that had happened with Jefferson, including the abuse, both verbal and physical. "It got awful. I began to think that Jefferson was evil and he might kill me."

"What an asshole. Why didn't you kick the shit out of him?"

"You know I'm not like that. I hate violence and confrontation of any kind."

Joey shook his head, lost for words. The breakup Shayne had endured was far worse than the one he had with JJ.

"There is good news." Shayne offered.

"Oh? Tell me."

"I got a modeling gig, Joey, and it's a good one. I've been hired to represent Versace's new cologne, Uomo, in a commercial. It will be shown all over North America and parts of Europe. I'm going to make sixty thousand dollars."

Joey whistled. "That is awesome, Shane. Finally, you got your break in modeling. You deserve it."

"Thanks," Shayne said, as their meals were delivered.

Two hours later, they had talked about everything the two of them were doing since Key West, and Joey said he had to leave because it was getting late, and he had a client in the morning. Shayne still didn't understand why he was working, considering he had that amount of money in his bank account. Joey claimed that it gave him something to do.

Both had things to do for the rest of the week, but promised to get together for a drink at Joey's apartment. Shayne was eager to see it, as well as the Ferrari, and made Joey promise to take him for a ride in it. Joey said he would, since Spring was just around the corner. They could take a weekend and go anywhere Shayne wanted. Shayne was thinking about heading up north to Muskoka, also known as "cottage country." It was a stunning showcase of some of the finest scenery Ontario had to offer. Shayne was sure Joey would love it, and it was the perfect lovers' getaway. Joey said he would look into it.

As they were set to part ways, Joey asked Shayne to follow him into the restroom, and once they were alone, he embraced him, delivering the most passionate kiss Shayne had ever received.

Outside of the restaurant, they lingered for a moment, then Joey walked across the street. Shayne watched him disappear into his building. He took a deep breath and went to find a cab.

CHAPTER 7
Spring in the City

The month of June arrived, and the temperatures were a balmy 69 degrees, but it felt even warmer. Gone was the snow that once covered nearly everything in and around the city, giving way to foliage that was sprouting and reaching for the sun's rays. The roads were finally clear of the harmful sand and salt that could damage a car, and Joey was itching to take the Ferrari out for a drive. He could finally put the top down and let his hair fly about in the wind.

In recent weeks, Joey and Shayne had rekindled their friendship, which felt almost like a relationship, though they hadn't become an official couple. Joey had known Shayne for nearly two years, including their time in Key West, but they still hadn't slept together. Always something prevented it—never another person, but work commitments ate their time. Currently, Shayne was deeply involved in the Versace shoot. He had no time for Joey, who understood because this was a once-in-a-lifetime opportunity that could significantly impact his modeling career. It would make it or break it, and Joey was hoping for the latter.

The first ride in the Ferrari would be solo. Joey pulled the cover off the car and stored it in the trunk of the Camaro. He hadn't started it in over two months and hoped he didn't have a dead battery. When he turned the key, it roared to life. Joey gripped the steering wheel, feeling its power flow through his hands. He was wearing his summer clothes, which he brought from the Keys: jeans, sandals, and his favorite loose-fitting muscle shirt that showcased his well-defined upper body with impressive muscles. Since he had nothing else to do besides his massage business, he started using the spa area of his building, which housed a full gym, stationary bikes, a sauna, and a swimming pool suitable for laps. His workouts had paid off, and he was in better shape than he had been when he lived in Key West. He also used the tanning beds located in a room just outside the gym. He had regained his golden tan as well. Overall, he looked the part of a man ready for summer, and sitting in the Ferrari made him feel like a rock star.

He put the car in gear, backed up, then drove up the exit ramp onto the Esplanade, turned right, then left onto Church Street. It wasn't long before he was noticing people staring at him from all directions. And why not? An extremely hot-looking man with long hair and a tan, driving a Ferrari. He was the envy of many people, both men and women.

His first stop was in front of Dino's, where he pulled up and parked in the loading zone. He caught Claire's attention and waved. She came out immediately.

"What the heck, Joey!" She exclaimed, looking at the car, then at the man sitting in it. "Wow!'

"Pretty sweet, huh?"

"Duh. And look at you all tanned and looking gorgeous."

“Oh, stop it.” Joey laughed.

A man passing by overheard her. "You know, she's right," he said and then kept walking.

“I can’t stay and talk, Joey. It’s busy today. Maybe later? Shayne has been so busy that I rarely see him these days. It would be nice to hang with a friend for a change.”

“When do you get off?”

“I got two hours left.”

Joey looked at his watch, and it read 1 pm. “Cool, I’ll pick you up here at 3 PM. We’ll go for a drive somewhere and maybe get a drink or a bite to eat. Cool?”

“Very. See ya then!” Claire went back inside.

Joey drove off, deciding to take the car out onto the highway.

As he drove, he glanced in the rearview mirror and admired his new sunglasses that he had bought at the mall. They were Ray-Bans, and he thought the aviator style suited him well. He also began to think about his and Claire’s relationship, which had grown substantially since their first meeting in Dino’s. He liked the girl. She was witty, funny, and brilliant, which made him wonder why she was still waitressing and not doing something more. She also was not dating anyone and hadn’t been since he had known her. He knew that she was a lesbian and that there were hundreds, if not thousands, of potential suitors for her in the city. Still, she remained single, and as far as he knew, all of her friends were gay men. Shayne had once kidded her, calling her a "fag-hag" for hanging out with gay men all the time. She just stuck her tongue out at Shayne, and that was the end of it. Still, Joey wondered if there was more to it than that.

The afternoon sun glimmered on the blacktop as Joey merged onto the highway and headed north, windows down, radio humming a familiar tune. He let the wind tangle his hair and tried not to think about Claire or the subtle ache that he felt from Shayne's absence. Two hours—just enough time to get lost in thought. He decided to drive up to Aurora and see if he could find David's old house. He chose not to keep it, and it had sold quickly. Apart from that, he drove without a care, letting the landscape blur past. The promise of conversation, of laughter, of old stories rekindled, buoyed his spirit. Sometimes, a simple drive was all it took to remind him that the world still offered small adventures, waiting at the turn of the next bend in the road.

He found the house simple enough, and it looked the same: a different car in the driveway and new curtains in the windows. He thought that if he walked up and rang the doorbell, he might be greeted by a smiling David opening the door. He missed David and his ways. However, he didn't stop for long. With an hour left before he needed to pick up Claire, he made a quick stop to fuel the Ferrari and grab a Diet Coke, then headed back toward the city. He would arrive on time to pick her up, but with little room to spare, as it was a 50-minute drive. He pushed the Ferrari a little over the speed limit to save time and soon was going 130 km per hour—fast, but not enough to get pulled over, as traffic was moving nearly at the same speed. There was also no rush hour traffic since he was heading into the city, not out. The traffic on the other side of the highway was increasing.

It was 2:55 PM when Joey pulled the Ferrari up to Dino's and a waiting Claire, who hopped in, dropping her purse at her feet.

"So, where to?" Joey asked.

She thought for a moment, then said, "I know of a little place in Mississauga. We can get a bowl of chili and a cold beer there. Also, if it's okay, I need to swing by my parents' house and pick up some mail. It won't take long, I promise."

"No sweat," he replied and sped off, thinking to himself, "Chili?"

Shayne was tired and grateful that the day was nearly over. He was starting to wonder about the countless takes the director was doing to get the scenes just right. Each one seemed to blur into the next, and his one line was getting tiresome. He truly believed he would never have to say, "Uomo, the scent to die for," again once this was over. There were only two days left to finish the commercial, and the people from Versace did not want the shoot to exceed the allotted ten days. Shayne wasn't worried about that. They were very happy with him—his looks and how he handled the role. To them, he was the perfect person to represent the Uomo brand, and he had overheard talk of another commercial featuring a different cologne that they might use him in. For now, Shayne was happy to get this one done and have some time off. He missed Claire and especially Joey's company. Once this shoot wrapped up, he would have three days off before the next shoot for the print material began. He kept reminding himself of the big check coming his way.

An assistant adjusted the loincloth Shayne was wearing, backed away, and the director yelled, "Action!"

Chris Lauden looked miserable, and it was visible all over his face as he sat across from his long-time girlfriend, who had just come across a receipt that had fallen out of his jeans pocket. It was Joey's advert from NOW Magazine. He had tried to explain that he was seeing a massage therapist because of back spasms, but with each excuse, he dug his grave deeper. She had done some detective work of her own, having a friend call this Joey to find out what it was all about. What she discovered shocked and pissed her off. Her boyfriend might as well have been seeing a male prostitute as far as she was concerned, upon learning what a happy ending was. Unable to get him to confess, she slapped him across the face, picked up her suitcase, and walked out.

Chris didn't think he was gay. Maybe bisexual: he still liked girls, although things hadn't been going well with his now-ex-girlfriend lately. Things had become strained as they spent more and more time apart, not necessarily with Joey, but he had started going to bars like Komrads and even Chaps, where he discovered male dancers. It was then, watching them gyrate their naked bodies on stage, that his attraction to men was stronger than he had first believed. He acted on it when he found Joey's ad. So far, the only thing he had done with a man was to get a hand job. Now, with her out of his life, he intended to explore his sexuality more deeply. He read about bathhouses where men went to socialize. That was his next step. He felt that his secret was finally partially out in the open, and if his Ex would be the bitch he thought she was, their mutual friends would soon know as well. "Fuck 'em." He thought. He could make new friends.

Chili, as Joey found out, was always the special at the bar Claire had brought him to. A sign outside featured a caricature of a cowboy holding up a bowl in one hand and a spoon in the other, and the name of the place was aptly named Chili's. Inside, Joey saw that the place featured a bar with tables in the front and a large dance floor toward the rear. Off to one side of it stood a mechanical bull, ready for its next cowboy to try his luck. A few hay bales were placed around Chili's, as well as other items denoting that it was a country and western establishment. They chose a table in the front that overlooked the parking lot and Joey's Ferrari.

"My dad used to bring Shayne and me here when we were kids," Claire explained. "During the day, it's open to everyone, but later on, when the dance hall opens, it's 19 years and older. I love the chili served here, which comes in several different styles and varying levels of spiciness. The three-alarm is very spicy."

Joey listened carefully to her as he looked over the menu. True to her word, there were six different types of chilies—some with meat, some vegetarian—all offering a choice of beans: pinto, baked, black, and more. Joey chose the Tex-Mex, medium with pinto beans, and

Claire decided on the same. They both ordered a beer; he chose a Blue, and she opted for a Lite.

"Why do lesbians always drink Lite beer?" Joey asked, remembering that the brand was the choice of most of the gay girls he had met in Key West.

"Miller is a gay friendly company, so I chose it over others, I guess. And the other girls in Toronto tend to drink it as well. I do like others like Molson and Labatt for Canadian Beer, but most of the time I choose Lite if they have it."

"Cool. I never did like Miller products. When I started to drink, it was Bud, then Michelob, which is Anheuser-Busch."

"I've heard bad things about Anheuser being very anti-gay. I could be wrong. Things like discrimination against different people, including gay people, such as not hiring them."

"I've never heard anything about it," Joey said, taking one of the complimentary chips from a bowl that sat on the table.

"Tell me how you feel about Shayne," She asked, munching on a chip and washing it down with a drink of beer. "Do you like him?"

"What kind of question is that? I love him."

"Love him like a close friend or…" She paused, hoping Joey would finish the sentence for her.

"What are you fishing for?" Joey asked. "Ok, back when we met in Key West, we hit it off the very first time we met at the Sea Isle Resort. I found him incredibly attractive, and I think he thought the same way about me, but we never took it to the next level. I had met an attractive doctor, and he eventually got involved with Jonathan. Then, we lost track of one another after we both left the island."

"So, how about now? Is there a chance of you two becoming a *thing?*"

"There is always a chance. We've been reunited now for what, a few months? I think we're just getting reacquainted with each other. Do I love him enough for a relationship like that? The answer is, I think I do. Vague, I know, and I am sorry. I suppose I'm not sure if he's ready after that nasty breakup he went through. I need to get more signals from him."

"You know what I think?" She was moving back as the waitress had come and set down two steaming bowls of chili in front of them.

"Refills on the beers?" She asked.

"Sure," Joey said. "Make it two Lite beers, please," Joey said, smiling at Claire.

The waitress left, and Claire leaned forward again. "I think you two are madly in love with one another, and both of you are too stubborn to admit it. I know for a fact that Shayne would practically die for you, and I think you would do the same for him. Tell me I'm wrong."

Joey picked up his spoon and stirred the chili with it, then looked at Claire again. "I guess my secret is out. I need to find a way to tell him that I am in love with him."

Claire gave Joey a grin that bordered on looking evil. "Leave that to me."

"Matchmaker." Joey put a spoonful of chili into his mouth, his reaction priceless to Claire. He looked like someone had just taken his tongue, placed it on the table, and hit it with a hammer.

"Ho…ho…hot!" Joey managed to say something and gulped down his beer, which only spread the heat, making things worse.

"You could have warned me that the medium was that hot. They should rename it Hades for Christ's sake. I owe you one, you little bitch." Joey was smiling in between bites of the fresh bread that had been served with the chili. Now he knew why. It was the only thing that would sop up and cool his mouth down.

Claire sat, not answering, humming along to the music on the radio.

CHAPTER 8
The Barracks

It had been a couple of weeks, and the weather was slowly heating up, making it warm enough to take the trip to Northern Ontario. Shayne had finished his first modeling shoot but still hadn't been paid. He had learned that the client was very demanding when it came to deadlines and when they wanted the project finished, but when it came to paying, it was another story. Another model had told him that he needed to keep getting work and "fill the pipeline" so that checks would come in regularly. The first one could take a month to be cut. Shayne was disappointed to learn about the policy, but he had enough money saved and could wait for the large check he was expecting. It seemed that all of the modeling industry followed the same snail-paced methods of paying their hired talent.

Joey and Shayne remained close friends, with Joey feeling their bond was strengthening over time. Claire's promise to do some matchmaking had not yet materialized.

Shayne mentioned he would like to take a trip together, and Joey looked into it. Muskoka was a two-and-a-half-hour drive north, and there were plenty of hotels available. As he dug deeper, he found a gay guest house that two lesbians ran. The lodging seemed perfect for them. He just needed to clarify when Shayne could go. As he had completed the modeling gig, he guessed that any time would be okay for him, but it was better to ask. He could do so that evening as they had a date for dinner at Joey's apartment. He did call and tentatively reserved a suite for the following weekend, including the Friday leading into it. The pictures of the place were very intriguing, as the house appeared to be decorated with antiques and other artwork that he presumed were from the area.

Joey finished his shower and got dressed for his upcoming client, scheduled to arrive soon. Chris was becoming a regular, but he was somewhat tiresome, as during his last visit, he couldn't stop talking about his breakup with his girlfriend and his newfound interest in men. Joey wasn't sure if Chris was just insecure or flirting with him. Regardless, he didn't care. It was Chris's choice of what he did, and Joey wasn't interested. He popped a bottle of oil into the microwave and went to get fresh towels.

Patrick Thibadeau paid $50.00 and entered The Barracks for the first time. The 19-year-old French Canadian moved from Montreal to Toronto to attend the School for the Performing Arts, aiming to improve his acting skills. With black hair and brown eyes, he came from a wealthy family and kept his sexuality secret, fearing his family would find out he was gay. He wouldn't be surprised if his mother hired a private investigator to keep an eye on him and report back. He had to be cautious when visiting a place like this, using his heavy winter clothing to conceal himself during the cold months. Now that summer was approaching, he no longer had that clothing to hide his identity.

He accepted the towel and room key from the attendant, who stood behind a glass partition at the front desk, and was directed to the location of the private rooms. He walked through a courtyard and around a swimming pool where a few men swam, naked and frolicking with one another. He walked past it and down a hallway. He checked the plastic red tag attached to the key. The number 3 was printed on it. He found the room, the matching number hand-painted on the door, and unlocked it.

Inside the small room, the furniture was minimal—just a full-sized bed and a table with two towels on it. Patrick undressed, folded his clothes, and placed them on the table. Wrapping a towel around his waist, he exited to explore the bathhouse, locking the door behind him, the key slipped onto his wrist.

Other than the pool, he had no idea of what was in the labyrinth that made up The Barracks' interior, so he set off to find out.

The first thing he noticed was in the locker room. What looked like twelve closets, six standing back to back and each with a door. He opened one of them, revealing a stool and a hole drilled waist-high in the wall. He closed the door, deciding he didn't want to try the glory hole. Not yet anyway.

The next room was spacious and very dark, requiring a moment for his eyes to adjust. He identified what resembled a back area typical of a leather bar. He saw the shapes of men interacting and a few wandering around, observing or waiting. Moving further, he entered the sauna. The hot room was humid, with water dripping from the tiled walls onto the lava rocks. Inside, only one man was present, leaning back with his eyes closed. Patrick took a seat.

The man was attractive, with brown hair that fell to his shoulders and appeared to be in good shape, neither too heavy nor too skinny. As Patrick adjusted himself on the wooden bench, the man opened his eyes, revealing his hazel eyes.

"Hi, I'm Chris." He said.

Patrick didn't think that this was the place for handshakes. "Hi. I'm Patrick." He replied, smiling.

"You have a room?" Chris asked, placing his hand on Patrick's thigh.

Patrick nearly gasped but maintained control, feeling his cock twitch under the towel. "Yes."

"Cool. Let's go."

Patrick stood up, unsure of what else to do, and followed Chris to his room, where their towels were quickly discarded. Being a submissive bottom, he let Chris take control and soon found himself lying between his outstretched legs, sliding his tongue up and down Chris's seven-inch, rock-hard cock.

Chris was really enjoying it. He liked the look of the young kid when he entered the sauna, and once he said hello and found out he was French, he became more intrigued. He told the twink that he wanted to go to his room and have sex with him, although not in so many words.

He believed he had made his intentions clear, and Patrick had gone along with it easily.

The blowjob he was getting was far better than his girlfriend had ever given him. This guy was taking his time, making love to his dick.

The massage he had just received that night from Joey had made Chris even hornier, despite the exceptional hand job that he received. Now, he was with a guy and was about to have his first real sexual encounter with another man.

He grasped his lover's hair in his hand and began to fuck his mouth, each thrust pushing deeper until Patrick gagged, pulling back to catch his breath, then wrapping his mouth around the shaft again.

Chris moaned as Patrick sucked on the head, his tongue dancing and stabbing at the piss slit.

"I love being your little sissy slut." Patrick said, pausing. "I want you to fuck me, and I want it hard and fast."

Chris looked at the boy between his legs, Patrick's face already covered in the saliva he was applying to his cock and balls. "Lick my asshole." He commanded.

Patrick eagerly complied, lathering the pink hole with more spit, trying to force his tongue inside.

"That's a good boy, now suck my cock some more. Make it like an iron rod. Yeah, like that. Pleasure your Master."

Patrick was using every bit of his skill to please Chris. He was aching to feel the cock he was sucking deep inside his asshole and was working hard to earn it. "Yes, Master, I love being your obedient fuck toy slave."

Chris was ready, and his cock was throbbing. He pulled the more petite teen up so that Patrick was straddling him. "Sit on that big cock and ride it, slut."

Patrick reached behind him, fumbling with the large shaft, and managed to get the large head positioned at his opening. Before he could sit down on it, Chris thrusted upward, burying his cock balls deep in Patrick's tight ass. Patrick let out a yelp, pain shooting through his body. Chris groaned, pleasure enveloping him. After a moment, the pain faded, and pleasure began to build in Patrick as he rode up and down using his muscles to squeeze the cock.

"Yeah, baby," Chris said, moaning. "Faster." He was letting Patrick do all of the work and just lay on his back watching him work, his face contorting with each time he buried the shaft into his body.

"Oh God, please take me and use me," Patrick begged. He desperately needed Chris to take control and fuck him. He didn't have to wait long.

Chris's orgasm was starting to build. He flipped Patrick over, pushing his head down into the pillow, pulling him by his waist so that his ass was in the air. He slapped his ass hard, leaving a red mark, then pushed his cock into the tight sheath. Both men groaned at the invasion of flesh into flesh. He began to pump in and out, Patrick pushing back, trying to force it in deeper.

Suddenly, Chris pulled out and went and opened the door before returning to stick his cock back into Patrick one again. He had the spur-of-the-moment urge to be watched while he fucked the little twink, and soon three men were standing at the door watching, their cocks in their hands, pumping in unison with Chris's thrusts.

"What are you doing?" Patrick asked.

"None of your business. Shut up and take it like the little femboy that you are." Chris responded by increasing the force of each thrust.

"Yeah, fuck that little bitch." One of the strangers said, and the others grunted their approval of what Chris was doing.

Patrick suddenly became aware that others were watching him. After a moment of panic, maybe of being discovered, he relaxed, his excitement growing as he realized that having a stranger watch him in intimacy was driving him to erotic heights that he had not been to before. "Oh, it's so big I can feel it in my throat." He moaned.

Chris was fucking Patrick's ass as hard as he could, his flesh slapping against him loudly. "I'm going to breed you, you fucking little whore."

"Fuck yes!!" Chris screamed, his orgasm washing over him with blast after blast of his hot cum coating the inside of Patrick's ass, who was frantically beating his cock, enclosed in his fist.

Chris finished and pulled out. He pushed Patrick onto his back. "Keep fist fucking your cock." He ordered, then looked at the men standing just outside the door. "Wanna cum on the slut?"

They didn't have to be asked twice and moved to surround Patrick, who was nearing his climax. Chris watched as the foursome came almost simultaneously. Patrick, all over himself, and one of the men came on his face, his mouth open to accept the cream—the others shooting all over his chest and stomach, drenching the teen.

Chris smiled and left; perhaps one of the 'booze cans' was open. It was after hours, the bars were closed, and he was in need of a drink. Throughout the city, illegal setups in empty apartments offered beer and liquor for those wanting to keep their party alive beyond nightclub hours. These places often moved locations, making them hard to find. The ongoing game between the police and the operators was a constant one. The "booze cans" not only sold alcohol but also illicit drugs. Chris was confident he could find one.

The men quickly left as well, one of them closing the door behind him. Patrick lay in a mixture of sweat and cum. He almost wished that the men had taken him as well and fucked him as Chris had done. He was sexually satisfied, and it had not been necessary. He needed to find the showers, clean up, and leave. He didn't want to be discovered and wanted to keep his secret guarded.

"Of course I want to go!" Shayne said ecstatically upon Joey's proposition of a mini vacation. "You are going to love it in Muskoka, and I can't believe that you booked us in a gay guest house as well."

"It's about time you two went on a honeymoon," Claire said, taking a sip of her root beer float.

Shayne stuck his tongue out at her.

The three met up for ice cream at a shop on Bloor Street, at the north end of Church Street. Popeye's was a favorite spot for gays and straights alike, and as usual, it was packed due to the warm temperatures. Besides ice cream, the store sold various types of coffee as well as donuts that were surpassed only by Tim Horton's, a donut chain owned by the famous Toronto Maple Leafs hockey player. Joey had initially intended to tell Shayne about the trip over dinner, but once again, something had gotten in the way. This time, it was a meeting Shayne had with his modeling agent about a new gig. He couldn't say no, so he went along with Joey's understanding of the dinner engagement and got the job. It was for the city promoting Centre Island and its amenities, as well as its beaches. It didn't pay anywhere near as much as the Versace job, but still, it would bring in enough money to support him for the foreseeable future. The shoot was scheduled for the end of the month, so Shayne had the time to go with Joey.

"Get this," Joey said, stirring in a teaspoon of sugar into his coffee. "The name of the guest house is The Frolicking Frog! How they came up with that is beyond me."

They all laughed at the name.

"I guess the men who stay there want to jump on one another?" Claire said, still laughing. Shayne nearly coughed up his coffee.

Neither Shayne nor Joey had commented on Claire's comment on their honeymoon, although they both had ideas.

"I think it's great that you two are finally finding the time to go away together. I'm going to miss you guys." Claire said on a more serious note.

"It's for three days, Kitten, "Shayne said.

"Kitten?" Joey was amused. "What's with the nickname?"

Shayne shrugged. "Just something that stuck when we were kids."

"I have an obsession with stuffed cats," Claire explained. "I have nearly five hundred of them at my parents' house."

Joey whistled. "Now that's a lot of pussy."

They all cracked up laughing again, and Joey's phone rang. He excused himself and walked off to answer it.

"This could be your big chance," Claire said once Joey was out of earshot. "He loves you, Shayne. He told me so."

Shayne eyed his friend. "So, you keep telling me. Are you sure he is ready after that breakup with JJ?"

"Ugh! When are you two going to get over the breakup excuse thing? He is worried about the same thing with you and Jonathan. For fucks sake, Shayne. Use this trip to tell him how you feel."

"I guess I can try." He said, looking at Joey, who was talking on his cell phone some ten feet away. "He is so incredible in so many ways." He said quietly.

"Even more reason to get your ass in gear. God only knows when he might make a move. You will both retire before you man up about your feelings." Claire sat back and crossed her arms, frustrated that she couldn't do more. She felt it was necessary to be careful not to be too pushy. Both men needed to make up their minds and do it in their own time. It would provide a solid foundation, honesty, and a basis for growth.

"I want to, Claire. I honestly do. It's just that every time I want to bring it up with Joey, something always comes up and gets in the way. Maybe this time will be different."

"Make it different this time, Shayne. Before something else gets in the way. Something like JJ."

Shayne sat back, Claire's words stinging him, bringing back the memories of regret. This time, it would be discussed, even if he had to be the one to do so. He watched Joey as he walked back, each of his steps sexier than the one before.

CHAPTER 9
Muskoka

Married men were visiting Joey more often and in greater numbers than usual. He speculated that the warmer weather might be a factor. He noticed that these men usually had secrets and felt compelled to confide in Joey. Each of them had a desire to explore his own sexuality with men. Sometimes, Joey wondered if he should charge them as a psychologist. Typically, he listened to their stories briefly, letting them pass through one ear and out the other, as his grandmother used to say.

Chris increasingly shared more about his coming out to Joey, with each visit feeling like an effort to gauge Joey's response. He was working up the courage to ask Joey out on a date, but hadn't done it yet.

Even if he did, Joey would politely decline, citing being in a relationship, even though he wasn't in one.

So far, a half dozen men had visited him over the last week alone, each one with their own stories, all of them swearing Joey to secrecy. As he showed Chris out, the man again asked Joey to keep quiet about their meetings together, and again, Joey swore he would. Joey still had his little secret, but he hoped to change that during his getaway with Shayne this coming weekend.

Shayne almost had to cancel plans with Joey when his agent called about another modeling job. This time, he declined, saying he had weekend plans he wouldn't change and could meet after he returned. She complained, warning that the job might be gone by then. Shayne didn't mind; his weekend with Joey was more important.

He kissed Claire goodbye as she left for work he finished packing his carry-on bag. It was small but would hold enough clothing for the three-day trip. He put his electric razor, two travel-sized bottles of shampoo and conditioner, and his toothbrush inside and zipped it shut. He checked his watch; Joey would pick him up soon. Despite it being only 7:00 AM, he swallowed the last of his port from a snifter. He felt jittery, but he knew he shouldn't. He and Joey shared a close bond, although it was not romantic. It was the prospect of intimacy that made him anxious.

Joey was on time, and Shayne was waiting for him on the doorstep when he pulled up in the Ferrari. He didn't need the car to make him look sexy, but Shayne had to admit, he fit it well. Joey might have been a rock star sitting behind the wheel, dressed in a muscle shirt and wearing his sunglasses. His hair was already a tangled mess as he had the top down, allowing the wind to toss and turn it.

"Sexy as hell," Shayne said to himself as Joey got out of the car and opened the trunk.

"All set to go?" He asked, giving Shayne a quick kiss on the lips.

"Yeah. Can we stop somewhere? I'm out of pads and just got my period this morning." He joked.

Joey smiled. "No need. That doesn't bother me at all. Just don't be a bitch."

"Gross." Shayne opened the door and sat down in the passenger seat, Joey closing the door after him, sat down, and turned the key in the ignition.

It was Shayne's first time in the Ferrari. Winter and the bad weather kept Joey from taking it out, and taking a drive never came up; Shayne didn't mention it other than that one time. Work and other things kept them from taking a drive together. Now, they had the time and the destination, and Joey was eager to show Shayne what his car could do. Ten minutes later, they were on their way up the 404 singing to "What a Feeling" by Irene Cara and having the time of their lives.

Halfway to Muskoka, it started to rain, and Joey pulled over to put the top up.

Shayne turned the radio down. "Dang weather," he complained, as he watched it slide securely into place.

"Hopefully it's just a passing shower," Joey said, double-checking that the rag top had closed properly. Satisfied, he turned back onto the road.

"What are we going to do when we get there?" Joey asked as he had never been there before.

"Well, there is a lot to do," Shayne began. "We can see if there is a festival happening, or maybe go to the theater? There are also numerous outdoor activities to enjoy. Hiking trails, boating, name it."

"I could go for a hike and see the scenery. The last time I did that, I was younger *and* in Maine." He admitted.

"I didn't bring proper boots, but there are stores all over where we can buy a pair."

"Maybe get a backpack and see what other gear we might need for a day trip."

"A canteen we will need for sure. There are streams I would drink from, however." Shayne said, turning the radio back on but keeping the volume low. "Fortunately, Canada's lakes and streams are not as polluted as some in the States."

"I know. Maine's waterways are still clean as well."

There are also markets where Native Canadians sell their wares. Some of the stuff is really nice."

Great, we'll take a look. Also, check out the hotel brochure from The Frolicking Frog that arrived in the mail yesterday. I put it in the glove box and haven't looked at it yet. Our reservation details are included there as well.

Shayne opened the glovebox and found it, then unfolded it.

"Anything exciting?"

"It says that the Frolicking Frog is located in the small township of Peekaboo Point. That's a cute name."

"It goes along with the name of the guest house, that's for sure. What else?"

"Let's see, there's a pool, although it doesn't specify whether it's heated or not, and there is a small restaurant."

"I think it's for guests only, and our meals are included with the package that I bought."

"There is a bar and a large fireplace. I assume the latter is meant for winter, though I'm unsure why anyone would visit then, except maybe for the small ski resort in Huntsville; there is not much to do."

"There is always ice fishing." Joey offered.

Calling the Huntsville ski area a resort was more of a joke as it was a single hill with a T-bar lift to reach its summit, which wasn't far. There were no mountains near Muskoka.

"Do you ski?" Joey asked.

"A little, but I'm not an expert. How about you?"

I'm an expert. I grew up skiing in Maine. I was even a member of the ski patrol when I was 18. It was just before I entered the service."

"Of course you were. Is there anything you haven't done? Skiing, scuba diving…"

"Oh, stop. I haven't done that many things. I have barely lived yet compared to some people."

"I guess. It's just that you have, at least to me, sometimes."

"Well, I haven't, but we have a lot of things to do together. I see a lot of fun for us in the foreseeable future."

Shayne fell silent and looked out the window. He was hoping that would be the case.

Outside was the Canadian wilderness. Dense woods now lined both sides of the road, which shrank to two lanes. The 404 stretched ahead as the Ferrari ate up the miles, then they turned onto 11. Soon, they would reach their destination.

A comfortable hush settled between them as the landscape rolled by in muted greens and golds. The Ferrari's engine hummed, seeming to echo the quiet anticipation that filled the small space. Shayne tapped the glass, watching the trees lean in and out of view, then turned back with a soft smile.

"Let's make a deal," he said quietly. "No more talk about what we have done. Let's say we'll do it all, new things, sooner than later."

Joey let out a small laugh, feeling the tension melt a little. "Deal."

Paul exited his doctor's office, feeling deflated and frightened after learning his HIV test was positive. Although his doctor minimized the results by mentioning that false positives are common, Paul was scared. He requested a second test, and the nurse drew his blood, with results expected in a few days. Paul was also angry. If he was positive, then he had gotten it from someone who was as well, and that infuriated him. Whether that person knew he had it or not, he must have had sex without the protection of a condom and hadn't realized it. His use of ecstasy would sometimes cause him to have lapses in judgment as well as memory. The other day, he had sex with someone at The Barracks, and try as he might, he couldn't even remember the guy's name or what he looked like. He knew for a fact that he hadn't gotten it from his now deceased lover. He had insisted on wearing a condom every time the two had sex together, and Paul had never cheated on him. If he *was* positive, then he had gotten the virus from someone during the past year.

When the second test came back positive, he was initially shocked, but the more he thought about it, the angrier he became. He decided that he was not going to be the only one to suffer from the dreaded disease. Someone was going to pay for infecting him, and he didn't care who it would be. It was time to visit The Barracks for some fun.

Claire was nearly finished with her shift when a woman at the bar smiled and beckoned her over. She responded with a smile and approached a blonde, blue-eyed woman, probably in her late twenties.

The woman was wearing clothing that resembled a business suit more than a typical dress, although it was fashioned as such.

"I'm Danielle," the woman said, offering her hand. "And you are?"

"Claire. Can I help you?"

"Maybe. I was wondering what time you get off and if you would like to have dinner with me tonight."

Claire stood there speechless. This woman had just asked her out on a date. "I, um…"

"I'm sorry for being so forward, but I usually go after what I want. I assume that you are family?" Danielle asked, taking Claire's hand.

"Yeah." Claire was having difficulty putting a sentence together, despite being gregarious.

Danielle noticed Claire's hesitation. "Let me start again. My name is Danielle, and I am a modeling agent and a lesbian. I think you are very attractive and would like to take you to dinner." She smiled and released Claire's hand. "Would you like to go?"

"Um, yeah, sure! That would be great." Claire still stumbled over her words.

"Great. How about tomorrow evening, around 8? I can pick you up at your place."

"Ok." Claire took her order pad and scribbled down her address as well as her telephone number, feeling fortunate that she was off the following day. She tore off the paper and handed it to Danielle, who opened her purse and slipped it inside.

Danielle then took the pad and pen and jotted down her number, giving the pad back to Claire. "Just in case you change your mind, or something comes up, then call me."

Claire tore off the slip of paper and stuffed it into her apron.

"Until tomorrow, then." Danielle stood, leaned over, and kissed Claire on the cheek, then left the restaurant and disappeared into the crowd.

Claire remained standing, leaning against a barstool, processing what had just happened. She just met the most beautiful woman she had ever seen and agreed to have dinner with her. She gave a stranger her address and phone number without a second thought. She hoped she wouldn't regret it. If only Shayne were here. She would trust her instincts.

A slow, nervous smile crept across Claire's lips as the bar gradually returned to its steady hum. The world seemed unchanged, but she felt transformed, as though a door she hadn't dared to approach had swung open quietly. She tried to focus on her shift, but her mind wandered: What would she wear? Could she trust this beautiful stranger?

On the way home, the streetlights wavered in the hazy dusk, and Claire clutched her bag close, the slip of paper with Danielle's number a tangible promise. She passed the thrift shop on the corner, its window filled with old paperbacks, and thought of how she found comfort in stories. She sought brave heroines at dusk instead of braving real adventures herself. Yet she was about to embark on one of her own.

Back in her apartment, Claire stood in front of her modest bookshelf, letting her fingers drift over the spines of her favorite novels for reassurance. She poured herself a cocktail, staring out into the quiet night, her thoughts a whirl of anticipation and self-doubt. For once, though, she resolved to let the unknown be thrilling rather than terrifying.

She jotted a quick note in her journal—just a few lines, a snapshot of the evening: "Took a chance. Said yes. Tomorrow, I let myself be open to possibility, just as I hope Shayne is doing tonight." Then, gently closing the cover, she let out a long, shaky breath and smiled, letting excitement settle in her bones. Outside, thunder rumbled, and rain began to splash against the windows.

Joey was enchanted with Muskoka upon their arrival. Muskoka was a large area comprising towns within the regional municipality. Their actual destination was on a lake, not too far from the 11 and the nearest town. The location was new to Shayne, as his family had spent their time on the far side of Lake Joseph; therefore, this trip would be a new experience for him as well.

The directions on the guest house's flyer were correct, and soon Joey was driving the Ferrari into a small lot in front of what appeared to be a Victorian-style, three-story house. Both Joey and Shayne found it somewhat odd to see such a house in the middle of the Canadian wilderness.

The house was red brick with green shutters and was beautifully landscaped with native plants, as well as stone walkways. A table was surrounded by Muskoka chairs, which Joey found nearly identical to the Adirondack chairs that he had grown up with. Next to them stood three flagpoles flying the Canadian, United States, and Union Jack flags.

Off to the side of the house was a dock with two more of the same chairs, and one end of the swimming pool could be seen just beyond a majestic red maple tree.

Joey opened the trunk of the Ferrari and removed their luggage. "Let's go check in, shall we?" He followed Shayne through a French-style door to the inside.

CHAPTER 10
The Frolicking Frog

Chris was beginning to enjoy his new life and being with the men he encountered at The Barracks, as well as a new leather bar he frequented called Boots. He discovered a new interest in BDSM to the point that he even bought a few pieces of leather to wear at the bar. His encounter with the twink at The Barrack bordered on an extreme form of sex without crossing the line. He thought he would enjoy tying that little whore up for a bit of punishment and fun. He hasn't encountered a young French Canadian since that encounter.

His new outfit featured a Muir cap, which had a rounded top and a small, stiff brim. He also had a pair of chaps which he wore over jeans, as well as a leather vest and black boots with silver buckles. After seeing them being worn in the club, he purchased a biker's wallet with a chain that attached it to his thick leather belt.

The ensemble made him feel differently about himself. He felt more in control of the things happening around him and gained the confidence to take control of others who sought to be controlled. Such was a young man he met at Boots. Chris could only describe the man as looking like he had before his coming out and his transformation. The man was okay-looking and came across as meek and shy. A perfect choice for what Chris had in mind, and after talking to him for a few minutes and learning that the man's name was Andy, he led him into the darkness of the back room.

The inside of The Frolicking Frog's front desk was set in what used to be the house's foyer, staffed by a full-figured woman in her forties dressed in a vibrant outfit of yellows, blues, and greens. She greeted Joey and Shayne warmly.

"Hi there! You must be Joey and Shayne." She said, opening a ledger on the counter in front of her. "DeeDee and I have been expecting you. Are you on your honeymoon?" She asked.

Shayne shook his head no.

"Oh, ok then. It's just that you chose the honeymoon suite, so I assumed…"

"No. Not yet." Joey said, smiling at Shayne, then at the woman. "I just wanted your best room as this is our first vacation together."

"Perfect. I'm Darla, one of the owners here. Welcome to The Frolicking Frog. DeeDee, my wife, is preparing lunch, which is available from 11 AM to 1 PM. Dinner starts at 5 PM. All meals are served in the dining room through that door," she pointed to her right, which was also the only other door in the foyer besides the entry. "Please sign here. Your credit card is already on file, so I won't need it at this time. It will be charged when you check out on Monday morning. Any questions?

Joey signed and said he had a few questions for her. At the same time, Shayne examined a rack of brochures sitting on one wall. He selected a few of them, then returned to Joey's side, who was receiving their key from Darla.

As they headed to their room, they both decided they liked Darla and wondered about DeeDee. They figured they would meet her later at lunch.

"Darn it," Joey exclaimed, unlocking the door to their suite.

"What?"

"I forgot to ask Darla how they came up with the name The Frolicking Frog."

Shayne laughed. "We'll find out later.

Claire called Danielle not to cancel but to ask what she would wear. She had no idea where this woman was going to take her. "Casual," Danielle said.

Even though Danielle wanted to keep the location a secret, she assured Claire that the place was nowhere near the caliber of a five-star but had great food and friendly staff. Claire sighed in relief and told Danelle that she would be outside her door at 8 PM.

"Make it 7 PM," Danielle said.

"Ok."

"See you then."

It had been a long time since Claire had to prepare for a date. This would be her first with another woman. She dated boys when she was younger and had spent a lot of her time with Shayne. She had always been attracted to other women, but got nothing other than a few friendships. She never slept with a woman and was nervous.

She mixed a Pearl Harbor for herself, hoping the vodka and Midori would calm her. Joey introduced her to the drink once when he was having dinner at Dino's. When the flavors of the melon mixed with the pineapple juice exploded in her mouth, she was instantly hooked and went out to buy the ingredients so she could make it at home. She made the cocktail frequently now.

She selected a pair of designer bell-bottom jeans, a 1960s retro style, paired with a tube top that accentuated her breasts. Checking her reflection, she saw that her nipples were slightly visible through the fabric. She also chose a pair of comfortable open-toed flat shoes. After a final glance at herself in the mirror, she stuffed the tips she had earned that day into her purse and went outside to wait.

The honeymoon suite, to Shayne's relief, was not decorated flamboyantly. Instead, the room consisted of three areas. The bedroom contained a king-size bed, two nightstands with table lamps and a phone, as well as a dresser with a chair and a mirror. Off the bedroom was a sitting area with a sofa, a coffee table, a loveseat, and a unit combining a TV and stereo. The bathroom was accessed through the bedroom and featured a shower stall, a large hot tub, and a wall entirely covered with a large mirror. The walls were painted in a light green pastel hue, and the floors were oak, shining in the sunlight streaming through three large windows that offered a spectacular view of Foot's Bay, one of Muskoka's many large lakes.

They dropped their bags on the floor, and Shayne jumped on the bed, stretching out to test its firmness. Satisfied, he rolled onto his stomach and looked at Joey, who had taken his shirt off.

Shayne admired his well-defined upper body, then said, "How come you don't have a tattoo? I mean, you were in the Navy. Don't all sailors get them?"

"No," Joey chuckled at the stereotype. "Some do, but I thought getting one was nothing more than scarring my body. I've worked hard to achieve this look. Why cover it with ink?"

"I see, I guess. So, what do you think?" Shayne asked.

"About what?"

"The room, silly. You are the one who picked it out. I wasn't even consulted."

Joey smiled. "Sorry about not including you, but there wasn't a lot of time to book something. As soon as Spring hits, it seems that these places begin to fill up. I didn't have much choice. As far as the room, I like it. I like it a lot. It's nicely decorated. I love the artwork, as well as the antique furniture. It's not plastic-looking like some places. It reminds me of Maine. Did you see that credenza out in the hall?"

"I did. It's beautiful."

"I guess the rest of the guest house is like this," he said, waving his hand around the room.

"Let's go find out," Shayne said, sitting up. "Didn't she say lunch was being made? I'm starved."

Joey chose another shirt from his suitcase to replace the muscle shirt that he had been wearing and slid the blue polo shirt over his head, then tucked it into his jeans. He took a moment to examine himself in the mirror.

"You are still the fairest of them all," Shayne said, recalling a line from Snow White. He then stood up and embraced Joey from behind. "And you are mine for the next couple of days."

Joey turned around and hugged him back, leaning forward to kiss him. "And you are mine. Now, let's go eat."

The restaurant that Danielle had chosen was not unfamiliar to Claire, and she had been there once before with a friend. "Together" was a lesbian owned and operated eatery as well as a bar that primarily featured live music. Its décor was lovely, and overall, the place was charming and welcoming.

Once the two entered, it became apparent that Danielle was a regular patron of Together as the waitress who came forward addressed her by name and asked her if she would like her regular table. She said yes, and they were led to a table near the stage where a young woman was setting up gear. Claire assumed she was the evening's entertainment.

"As you can probably gather from the greeting we received at the door, this is one of my favorite places to come. The food is wonderful and the entertainment first class." Danielle said, looking over the wine list. "May I?"

"Huh?" Claire asked.

"Choose a bottle of wine for us. Do you have a favorite?"

"Not really. A lovely Chardonnay, maybe?"

"Perfect choice. We will take a bottle with a wine chiller, please." Danielle asked the waitress. "And give us a few minutes to look over the menu."

The waitress smiled and walked off.

"So, you work at Dino's." It wasn't a question but more of a statement. "I'm sorry if I came on strong, but I was taken with your looks. You are very attractive."

Claire thought that Danielle was an aggressive woman, but it didn't bother her. She felt more at ease taking a more submissive role when it came to other women, and she hoped that her inexperience was not too evident. "It's ok, I don't mind. You will see that I am open and friendly once you get to know me."

The wine arrived, and the waitress poured them both a glass and left once again, affording them more time to decide on their dinner.

"I am looking forward to doing just that," Danielle said, holding up her glass. Claire held up hers, and they toasted. "To a wonderful evening," Danielle said.

Claire thought that a woman could not have sounded or looked sexier than the one sitting across from her. "To a wonderful evening."

"I'll take the chicken salad with a Diet Coke," Joey said to a young man who waited on them.

"I'll have the same." Shayne echoed.

The lunch menu offered only three options: a chicken sandwich on a freshly baked wheat roll, a chicken salad with a freshly baked roll and a pat of butter, or a two-piece fried chicken platter that included fries and a dollop of coleslaw.

"It seems that chicken is the choice of the day," Shayne said. "I wonder what is for supper. Chicken à la King?"

Joey laughed as the young man who looked more like a boy in his late teens arrived with two glasses, which he delivered, then zipped off to attend to another table. "It's not very busy, is it?"

A total of ten people had lunch. Four men sat together, along with two couples, each consisting of two men and two women, including Joey and Shayne.

"This is not a very large guest house, and it might not be at full occupancy." Shayne offered.

"Probably. I saw you take a couple of fliers. Anything interesting?"

"Oh, yeah," Shayne replied, pulling them from his back pocket. There were four of them, and he handed two to Joey. "I haven't looked at them yet, other than the cover. One appears to be some boating thing, another a dinner show, a theater production, and a mini-golf course."

"Cool. Looks like you gave me the dinner show and the boating. The show is a murder mystery, which sounds interesting, and boating is a sightseeing activity that mainly showcases nature. I'm not into doing that at all," Joey said, placing them on the table, making room for their lunch that had arrived.

"The Toronto School of Fine Arts is performing a production of CATS, so that might be good. I imagine that it's at a small venue. And the mini golf looks like a lot of fun. The place has three courses with waterfalls and the usual themed obstacles, like a windmill and tunnels—that sort of thing. Can we go play?" Shayne sounded excited about doing so.

"Sure, why not. We have the rest of today and two more. I'm up for the murder mystery tomorrow and maybe CATS the night after? What do you think?" Joey asked, taking a forkful of salad.

"Fine with me. What do we do during the day?"

Buy a pair of hiking boots and explore the local trails. I would say take a swim, but I'm not sure the lake is warm enough yet. We can check out the pool, though."

"You and your laps."

"You want me to keep my girly figure, don't you?"

Shayne smiled and took a bite of the roll he had just buttered.

An hour later, they were teeing off on a par three that offered three tunnels, only one of which guaranteed a hole in one.

CHAPTER 11
Chickpeas & Caviar

Joe Clute was jonesing for the touch of Joey's magical hands, but he was out of town taking a well-deserved mini vacation, so he had said during his last treatment. Thus, he was trying someone new from NOW Magazine. The masseur's name was Greg, and the way he had described himself was intriguing. A Scandinavian with large hands and a convertible cock was something that he just had to see for himself, and the man's price was identical to Joey's at a reasonable $65.00 for an hour. He wasn't as convenient as Joey, and he would have to take a cab over to Sherbourne Street, but the weather was pleasant, and if he had a problem hailing one, he would walk.

The building Greg lived in was also not as lovely as 25 The Esplanade, where he and Joey lived, and Joe's apartment was much smaller and had nowhere near the views of Joey's Penthouse. Once inside Greg's apartment, he found the Penthouse portion of his pitch to be a little misleading. Technically, it was a penthouse and was numbered as such; however, to Joe, it was no more than a one-bedroom flat on the top floor of a seven-story building.

"Welcome!" Greg had greeted Joe warmly. "I hope you had no problem finding the place?"

"Not at all," Joe answered.

"Good. Please come this way." Greg led him into the bedroom, where it was made up with towels to perform the massage.

Joe lay on beds before for massages. Some were adequate, others terrible. He pushed his hand into the mattress and found it acceptable.

"If you will please undress? You can place your clothes on that chair. I will be right back with a bottle of warm almond oil." Greg smiled and left the bedroom.

Joe stripped off his clothing and folded it neatly before placing it on the chair. He then lay face down on the bed, with his head at the foot of it and a towel covering his butt. He wasn't embarrassed about showing off his body, but he felt modest: this was the first time with Greg.

The hour passed quickly, and Joe toweled off and dressed. Greg had not offered to let him shower. He paid him the $65.00 and left, deciding to walk home. Greg had done a good job, but it was not up to the standards he was accustomed to with Joey. He wouldn't be making a second appointment with Greg.

Claire rested in Danielle's embrace, feeling the afterglow of her first experience with another woman. Despite Danielle's assertive manner in conversation, her bedside manner was soft and caring, making Claire feel genuinely valued. She hoped this would not be just a one-time encounter. Claire looked forward to sharing her feelings with Shayne once he returned from his trip.

Danielle used the tips of her fingers to lift Claire's chin and kissed her.

Shayne beat Joey in mini golf; Joey struggled to navigate obstacles and occasionally hit the ball off the surface. Shayne played with precision, making each hole seem effortless. All Joey could do was admit defeat and agree to the rematch Shayne was demanding. Their scores didn't change much from the first game.

"That's it for me," Joey said, turning in his putter. "I suck at this game."

Shayne put his putter down on the return counter as well and joined Joey as they walked to the car. "You did ok." He said apologetically.

"Yeah, right! Did you see what I did on the 4th hole? I hit it in the water, and that fountain was three holes over at least!"

Shayne laughed. "At least you yelled fore. So, what's next, lover boy?"

"Lunch somewhere, then we buy some hiking gear and hit the trails. I think I found one that goes along the lake. It starts next to the Frolicking Frog, according to the map I got at the front desk."

"I didn't see that," Shanye said, looking at the pamphlet that Joey pulled from his pocket.

"I asked if they had something showing hiking trails. You were still in the room getting ready. DeDe gave it to me."

"You met DeeDee. What is she like?"

"The exact opposite of Darla. In looks, anyway. She is as thin as a rail and tall."

"Was she nice?"

"Very. Just as much as Darla was. I guess they share the work around the guest house. She said that Darla was cooking today."

"Hopefully, not chicken." Shayne laughed.

They found a sporting goods store in the nearby town of Coutnac Beach, as Peekaboo Point didn't have one, and it sold everything the two needed for a day hike: boots, canteens, walking sticks, and items like bug spray to ward off the mosquitoes. Joey bought a topographical trail map to replace the pamphlet because it showed elevations and other details. They also opted for one backpack that Joey would wear to store their newly acquired rain gear and other items. Joey insisted on buying some trail mix, and Shayne was horrified. He despised the concoction of dried fruit, nuts, and assorted seeds. "You can eat that crap," He had said. "I'll stick to my Snickers bars."

Joey had responded with, "It's *your* waistline."

At lunchtime, both Joey and Shayne were pleasantly surprised by the meal, neither of whom had tried the salad before. The theme of the day was Mediterranean with a twist—adding a touch of the American Southwest. They were settling into the dining room and had consistently sat at the same table since arriving at the Frolicking Frog. It seemed other guests were also becoming more social and friendly, exchanging greetings, names, and hometowns. The female couple had flown in from England, with Muskoka being their third stop on a cross-country sightseeing trip across Canada. The foursome was from Toronto, and the two men were from South Florida, scouting the area for a possible summer cottage to buy.

"This salad is delicious," Shayne said, shoveling another forkful into his mouth. "I wonder what is in it?"

"Let's find out." He said, but before he could call the waiter, one of the men closest overheard Joey.

"It's quite delicious, isn't it?" he said, wiping his mouth with a napkin. "It is made with chickpeas, black beans, and other assorted vegetables. It's called Cowboy Caviar because it's a Mediterranean staple mixed with a bit of Texas, if you will. And there is no caviar in it."

"Thanks," Joey said, smiling. "It's delicious."

"And filling," Shayne added. "I can't eat another bite; I am so full."

"You can burn it off on the hike," Joey said. "Speaking of which, we need to get our butts in gear. You ready?"

"Ready, Freddy," Shane said and stood up.

"You two have a good time." The man chirped, and his partner said, "Ta-ta," as Joey and Shayne left.

"Lovely couple." One of the men said to the other.

Joey located the start of the trail just beyond the swimming pool. He couldn't help but stick his hand into the water.

"It's heated." He dried it on the new plaid shirt he had bought from the sporting goods store. Shayne had gone all out with the name-calling once he saw it: "mountain queen", "butch", "stud", and "macho Joey gave him a look and flipped him the bird.

After an hour and a half, they arrived at a stream that flowed from the dense forest into the large bay they had been hiking alongside. If taken by boat, the bay would eventually empty into Lake Huron. Joey crossed the stream and started walking again, but he heard a splash and Shayne cursing. Turning around, he saw Shayne sitting in the water after slipping, with water flowing around and over his legs.

"Shit. Given me a hand, please, Joey?"

Joey helped him up and onto the stream bank. "What happened?"

"I slipped," Shayne said, wringing the water out of his shirt tails. "I'm soaked."

Joey took a quick look at the map. "Well, we are nearly to the turnaround point, so we might as well head back from here. You, ok?"

"Other than my pride *and* my ass hurting, I'm fine. Let's go."

By the time they reached the Frolicking Frog, it was sunset, and they were just in time for dinner. After they changed clothes, they went down to see what was being served, and Joey was overjoyed to find that Maine lobster was on the menu along with clam chowder—neither of which he had eaten for a long time. He was going to savor every morsel of the meal.

"I want to do some laps after supper. Is that ok with you?" Joey asked as he buttered another warm roll.

"As long as you won't swim until midnight."

"Promise. I feel the need for a little exercise."

"But we just finished hiking!"

"And…?"

"Ok, I'm having no effect here. I'm going to explore the guest house while you swim. I saw that there are common guest areas, such as a library and a drawing room."

"Cool. We can meet up after and maybe have a nightcap at the bar."

"Ok." Shanye wasn't happy about the impromptu swim, as he wanted every waking moment, as well as when they were asleep, to be spent together. But he knew that Joey was a workout fanatic and cut him slack. He also felt guilty, as he hadn't set foot in a gym for a couple of months, and his body was starting to show the effects of the lapse. Working out would have to start being a priority now that his modeling career was beginning to take off. Shayne decided to have dessert as Joey walked off to the room to change. He was, after all, on vacation, so a little ice cream wouldn't hurt.

Paul had just finished with his third trick at The Barracks when the raid came. Without warning, police entered the bathhouse and quickly moved through it, arresting men as they went. Paul had just finished dressing and heard the commotion. He peeked out from his private room and saw a man wearing a towel being handcuffed. Paul quickly headed in the opposite direction toward the back of the building, found the emergency exit, pushed it open, and slipped away into the night. Either the police didn't bother guarding it, or they didn't know it was there.

As Paul rounded the corner, he could see police cars and a paddy wagon in front of The Barracks. He paused for a moment to watch as the Police escorted man after man, placing them into the paddy wagon. The owner was standing, watching his customers get arrested, although he was not in handcuffs himself. He was given a summons that would result in a hefty fine. Of those taken into custody, all would be released and the charges dropped, unless they had outstanding warrants, as some of the hustlers did. They would be facing a judge.

Paul had no outstanding warrants or fines, but he wanted to avoid any issues with the police. He saw no reason for such raids, which he suspected were mainly aimed at searching for drugs. To him, it also seemed like another effort to suppress gay rights, though part of it was also about controlling HIV and AIDS, which were widespread in the city and among some of the men they arrested. Paul was indifferent because he felt it was too late for him. Someone had infected him with the virus, and without a cure, he believed his time was running out.

He turned his back on the controlled mayhem and headed for home.

Joey had lost track of time as usual, and by the time he crawled out of the swimming pool, it was nearly 11 PM. Shayne had not come looking for him, so he figured that he was either pissed off or had lost track of time himself. Neither was the case.

As Joey walked into their suite, he found Shayne deep in sleep, clutching a pillow to his chest and snoring quietly. It seemed that the hike had taken more out of him than it had Joey.

He looked at Shayne in his slumber, then walked to the window and opened it. Outside, a warm breeze rustled through the gardens, carrying the faint sound of distant laughter and clinking glasses from the bar. The night seemed to pulse with possibility, yet also with a quiet melancholy that settled on Shayne as he stirred in his sleep. Joey, towel draped over his shoulder, paused for a moment beside the window, letting the moonlight spill across his body. He watched as well-placed torches flickered along a path that led from the pool, disappearing around the corner, and thought about how quickly moments could shift from lighthearted to heavy, and how fragile their sense of safety sometimes felt.

He tiptoed around the room, careful not to wake Shayne. On the table, a half-eaten bowl of ice cream was beginning to melt, a silent testament to Shayne's resolve to embrace vacation indulgence. Joey smiled, feeling oddly comforted by this mundane evidence, and wondered about the possibility of a shared life. He quietly set his phone to charge, slipped into bed beside Shayne, and closed his eyes, hoping that tomorrow would bring fewer distractions and more time together.

Dreams drifted in, mingling with the gentle hum of the air conditioner, until sleep claimed him as well. The night deepened, carrying stories into the silence, waiting to be written down or spoken aloud.

CHAPTER 12
Rings

Danielle dropped Claire off the following morning, promising to call her later in the day. She had to go to work; she was working on a deal for her modeling client that would take most of the afternoon. Claire had the day off for a change and decided to take her bike over to Centre Island. It would be her first trip of the summer to the piece of land that was accessible only by boat or by airplane. She would take the ferry.

She enjoyed frequent trips to the island whenever she had time. She loved the pier, which featured carnival game booths, fast-food vendors, and stunning views of *both* Toronto *and* Lake Ontario.

She also enjoyed the petting zoo and the floral gardens and wondered if Danielle might want to join her. There was also Centerville Amusement Park, which had rides they could enjoy together, but it wasn't a place to visit alone. She quickly dressed in something comfortable, took her bike, and headed off.

The sun was already warm on her shoulders as she pedaled through the leafy neighborhoods, the city's early bustle fading behind her. At the ferry terminal, families queued up with strollers and coolers, laughter and anticipation floating on the morning air. Claire bought her ticket and stood at the railing as the boat glided across the lake, the skyline shrinking behind her, the island spreading out in a tapestry of green ahead.

On Centre Island, the day unfolded gently. Claire wandered past cyclists and picnickers, pausing to watch children race along the boardwalk. The air was scented with sunscreen and fried dough. She played a round of ring toss at a faded booth, ate salty fries, and let herself feel, for the first time in weeks, the quiet thrum of contentment. Danielle had given her those feelings.

Later, she found a patch of grass near the edge of the pier and lay back, letting the sounds of the city drift away. Beyond the laughter and seagulls, she heard only the wind and the steady lap of water against the shore. Her mind wandered to possibilities: the chapters unwritten, the things that always seemed to hover just out of view.

As the afternoon faded and the sky began to blush with sunset, Claire gathered her things, boarded the return ferry, and felt her heart was lighter than it had been in a long time.

Joey didn't mention how late he had returned last night, and Shayne didn't ask. He wondered if Shayne was upset for falling asleep, though he also had regrets. The previous night was another chance for them to be intimate, and he felt he was the one who missed it. Many unintentional distractions prevented their relationship from progressing. Joey realized he could have skipped the swim that evening, and things might have turned out differently. "Tonight," he thought, "will be the night."

With only two nights remaining of their brief vacation, they planned to attend a murder mystery dinner theater that evening. The brochure said it would be held at The Bear's Claw restaurant in Midland, a twenty-minute drive away. It was scheduled to start at 7 PM and end at 10:30 PM, so Joey thought they would be back at the Frolicking Frog no later than 11. Plenty of time to have a couple of drinks at the bar, maybe buy a bottle of wine, and then relax in their suite for what he hoped would be a night of. For the day, they decided to go to an outdoor shopping bazaar being held in Peekaboo Point. Both wanted a fun and relaxing day.

As evening settled again over the city, Claire and Shayne moved through their separate orbits, each haunted by hopes and what-ifs. Sounds of the country and the city lights flickered across separate waters, tracing lines between distant windows and memories not yet spoken aloud. In these moments, when the day's noise faded, both found themselves reaching for solace in memories—sometimes their own, sometimes borrowed, always seeking a thread of meaning to guide them forward.

For Claire, the hum of her bicycle tires on the sidewalk and the echo of laughter from the island were now memories. For Joey, the promise of tonight was a silent vow, an anchor in the ebb of uncertainty. The world around them brimmed with stories—unfinished, urgent, waiting to be lived and retold.

Somewhere, in the hush between longing and fulfillment, new tales gathered shape, ready to spill onto fresh pages.

A lingering thought haunted Joey's mind. Just before falling asleep, he watched Shayne sleeping and felt deep inside that Shayne was the one for him. He took a ring, hidden in the fold of his wallet, and ran his fingers over the gold band set with a single emerald. The inside was engraved with "Forever, as one, we dream." Another ring, identical but smaller in circumference, remained in his wallet. The ring he held was meant for Shayne, should he accept it.

Joey was confident that the two would be compatible in intimacy; he believed the sex would naturally work out. He also had no doubts that they'd get along if they tried living together, as his past two years of knowing Shayne had shown that their habits and mannerisms aligned positively. Both were meticulous about cleanliness and passionate about working out, and they shared similar interests in activities and music. To Joey, they appeared to be an ideal match. Did Shayne feel the same way?

He planned to ask that very evening, after they made love, if Shayne would consider moving in with him. If he agreed, he would then give Shayne rings—not wedding rings but rings of endearment that would bond them together. A wedding, if everything went as planned, might take place later, possibly in Las Vegas, where it was legal.

He would find out the following night. He placed the ring into his wallet and went to bed.

James had been having trouble with his wife lately. She found Joey's ad in her husband's pants pocket before washing them. It wasn't the whole page from NOW Magazine, so she had no idea where it came from, but she didn't care. The headline on the small piece of paper made her wonder. 'Man4Man' wasn't your usual advertisement for a massage therapist. There was something not right, and she would speak to James that evening. In the meantime, she would call this Joey and learn what might be going on during these Man4Man massages.

That morning, the sun poured softly into their suite, casting golden latticework across the tangled sheets and bare shoulders. Outside, the air buzzed with the promise of market stalls, fresh coffee, and the gentle clatter of people who believed in weekends and good luck. Joey rose first, brewing a pot of coffee and letting the aroma drift toward Shayne, hoping to ease the slight tension he thought might linger between them.

They dressed casually, laughter returning as they debated whether hand-knit scarves or local honey was the better souvenir. The bazaar unfurled before them: vibrant stalls heavy with wildflowers, worn books, and hand-thrown pottery. A busker played old jazz, his hat collecting coins and good wishes, while children spun in the near distance, their joy contagious. Joey and Shayne drifted from table to table, their conversation light, but for Joey, it was underpinned by the gravity of what he carried in his wallet.

By noon, they had gathered a bag of treasures—artisan soap still dusted with lavender, a map of nearby hiking trails, and a set of vintage postcards Shayne insisted would look perfect on his fridge. They paused for lunch beneath the awning of a café, sharing slices of tart lemon cake and stories from their pasts, as if laying out threads for a tapestry they might someday call home.

"I haven't thanked you for bringing me on this trip, Joey."

"What's to thank? I want to spend time with you, and this seemed like the perfect way to do it. Are you enjoying yourself?"

"Except for taking unexpected plunges into cold streams, yeah," Shayne replied, washing down a bite of cake with his coffee. "Are you?" He searched Joey's face, wondering if he was.

"There is no one I'd rather be here with, Shayne. You should know that. You should also know how much I love you." Joey said, testing Shayne's reaction.

"I love you too," Shayne said nervously, then looked down at his coffee, stirring it.

An awkward moment passed before Joey reached into his pocket, pulled out his wallet, and opened it. He rifled through it, his fingers touching one of the rings and lingering on it before taking out a twenty-dollar bill and placing it on top of the check. "That should cover it," He said, then put his wallet away. "How about we head back?"

"Sure," Shayne said and finished off his coffee that had gotten cold.

They walked back through the lively market, arms brushing, as the late sun cast a honeyed glow over the narrow city streets. The earlier tension seemed to have faded into the flow of daily life, replaced by small hopeful glances and a subtle sense of possibility. At a corner flower stall, Shayne stopped, captivated by a cheerful array of peonies and snapdragons. Joey watched as Shayne chose a single, pale flower, pressing its cool stem between his fingers. "For luck," Shayne said, and tucked it behind Joey's ear. Joey laughed—perhaps a little too loudly—but neither of them minded.

Their drive to the guesthouse was slow, carrying the comfort that only comes after secrets are shared, or nearly shared. The sky above the rooftops shifted from blue to amethyst. They paused on the Frolicking Frogs' old stone steps, listening to a distant train and the rustling leaves. Inside, the room was quiet, broken only by the faint hum of the air conditioner.

By the time Shayne appeared, with damp hair and cheeks flushed by the sun, Joey had placed the flower in a glass of water beside the bed. "Shall we?" he asked, voice more steady than he felt. Shayne nodded, slipping on his watch. Their hands naturally found each other, as if answering a question neither had dared voice. Outside, evening approached, and their story slowly, gracefully, moved toward what would come next. As the afternoon waned, anticipation for the evening's dinner theater grew. They exchanged quiet smiles and promises of a night unlike any other. Joey had rehearsed his words in the mirror, fingertips brushing the outline of the ring.

Later, as they were getting ready to head to the theater, Shayne was lying on the bed, flipping through a slim novel borrowed from the guest house library. He caught Joey's eye and grinned silently, suggesting that perhaps the future was closer than either of them dared to admit.

With dusk settling over the lake and headlights stretching toward Midland, they chatted, conversation turning to laughter, toward chance, and toward the kind of love that might, with care, rewrite everything that followed.

Claire's day on Centre Island was, as she expected, wonderful, and she felt a twinge of sadness when leaving. Once home at her townhouse, she had a light snack and then settled onto the couch with a book she had recently purchased. The cover showed two attractive women embracing, and the title held meaning for her: *Hidden Secrets to Make a Lesbian Relationship Work*. After reading through chapter three, she decided the book wasn't quite right for her; it read more like a novel than a helpful guide for a growing relationship. Its clichés made her feel nauseous. The author's name also seemed unlikely and probably a pseudonym. Carla Creamwell sounded too funny to Claire. She closed the book but kept it alongside her other books on a nearly full shelf, all of which she had read at least once. This book would remain the only one she wouldn't revisit.

It was nearing 5 PM when her phone rang, and she jumped to answer it.

"Hi, this is Claire."

"Hi, beautiful." It was Danielle. "What are you doing?"

"I was reading a book that I bought, but it sucks, so I put it away. How about you?"

"I just closed the deal for my client, and it looks like he is going to do well on this one, which means I do well. How about you go out with me and celebrate?"

"Love to! Where?"

"I don't know yet. Pick you up in half an hour?"

"Make it an hour and it's a date."

"See you then."

Claire hung up, threw her hands up.

After ending the call, Claire glanced at her reflection in the hallway mirror, smoothing her hair and grinning at the anticipation of the evening ahead. She selected a favorite shirt—soft blue linen, easy and welcoming—and a pair of dark jeans, then opened her jewelry box to choose a simple pendant, something understated but special. The next hour slipped by quickly as she refreshed her makeup, fed her cat, and pondered where Danielle might take her. When the doorbell chimed, Claire felt a flutter in her chest.

Danielle stood on the stoop, her smile radiant, hair perfectly tousled. She wore a blazer over a crisp white tee and held out a single sunflower as a greeting. "Ready for a little adventure?" she asked.

"As long as you're leading the way," Claire replied, tucking the flower behind her ear as they laughed together and descended the steps.

The city outside buzzed with the anticipation of summer. They wandered down the street, engaging in a relaxed chat about books, classic movies, and their neighbors' oddities. Danielle proposed they begin at Woodbine Beach, which was walking distance from Claire's townhouse, and Claire gladly agreed, happy with the spontaneous plan. As they strolled, Claire shared her frustration with her recent book, and Danielle joked about creating their own relationship guide—one filled with more genuine moments and laughter rather than clichés.

By the time the sun dipped low, they'd found themselves at a tiny café, half-hidden by climbing ivy, where they shared pastries and stories until the sky grew violet. Later, after heartfelt goodbyes and lingering smiles, Claire returned home, her heart buoyant.

She surveyed her bookshelf, eyeing the dubious paperback among her well-loved titles, and thought, with a private grin, that perhaps some stories were best written in real time. Then, with a sense of contentment, she began to rearrange her books—placing a few favorites beside the odd ones, letting her collection grow as unpredictably as her adventures.

The evening ended with neither Joey nor Shanye guessing who the murderer was, both thinking it was the valet with a tire iron. It had turned out to be a handyman with a hammer. The dinner was good, although Joey opted not to eat the prime rib and settled for the salad, baked potato, and steamed vegetables. Shayne thought Joey was crazy for turning down such a meal and ate all of his. Joey thought eating it rare was gross.

As they drove home, neither spoke much, except to discuss the show and express their enjoyment of it. Joey was once again thinking about the rings in his wallet, and Shayne wondered if this would be the night *it* finally happened. He leaned back in the seat, closing his eyes and resting his hand on Joey's thigh. Joey looked at it and smiled.

CHAPTER 13
Wherein Lies a Secret

"It's your wife again on line two," James McCormick's secretary informed him. It was her fifth attempt to reach him, and his excuses were starting to run out. He knew what she was calling about and wanted to avoid another argument. The initial one they had had the night before was bad enough.

As the bank's vice-president, he had more things to deal with than he had time for in a day. The last thing he needed was to spend time fighting on the phone with his wife.

He was angry with himself for being so sloppy. Usually, he was a well-organized man who took pride in not leaving loose ends that could result in financial losses. He was, after all, a financial specialist. However, he made a significant mistake. Leaving Joey's advert from NOW Magazine in his pants pocket might just cost him his marriage.

He let out a tired sigh, rubbing his temples and glancing at the blinking light on his phone. The office, with its polished wood furnishings and a faint scent of old paper, felt more like a gilded cage than a place of authority. James stared out the window, watching the reflection of city lights flicker in the glass, each one a reminder of promises made, and secrets carefully stowed away.

He stood, restless, and wandered to the bookshelf behind his desk. Rows of hardcover novels and bank policy binders lined the shelves, but his hand lingered over a collection of mystery stories—a quiet rebellion amidst the order. He traced the spine of a favorite, half-tempted to lose himself in a world where puzzles could be solved with wit and determination, unlike the tangled knots of his own life.

The phone rang again, persistent, insistent. James hesitated, then finally picked up, bracing himself for another round. As the conversation began, his gaze drifted to the bookshelf, where the titles seemed to whisper of far-off coasts, haunted manors, and adventures waiting just beyond the horizon.

He reached over and pressed a button, activating the speakerphone. "Yes, Rebecca," What is it now?" He said.

Instead, the burst of an expected angry soliloquy, the voice of a sobbing woman filled his office, followed by "I want a divorce."

An hour later, he had managed to calm her enough so she would listen. His excuse for having the ad was to give it to Joe, one of his gay employees. He explained that he found the advert while having coffee, leafing through the latest issue of NOW Magazine, which was the only thing available in the coffee shop. As he was eating his morning bagel, he came across the ad quite innocently. Joe, who was openly homosexual, had been complaining of a bad back and thought this might help him. "After all," he told his wife, "an unhappy employee isn't productive and isn't a positive asset to the bank." Her sobbing subsided into sniffling. He ended the call by promising to take her out for dinner and discuss the matter further if she wished to do so. She agreed.

He hung up and had his secretary make a reservation at Chez Voila, the most expensive and lavish restaurant in Toronto. Her favorite meal, accompanied by a costly bottle of wine, could help ease the gravity of the situation. He hoped he could thaw things between them and thicken the ice beneath his feet.

James called his secretary once more and told her he was stepping out of his office for a short while and to take messages. He needed to find Joe and let him in on what was happening with his wife. There was a chance she might come by the bank to search for and find Joe to get his side of the story. He would nip that possibility in the bud right now. There would be no more loose ends.

Joey moaned as he rode up and down on Shayne's hard cock, balancing himself by placing his hands on Shayne's muscular chest. He leaned forward and kissed him, exploring his mouth and teeth with his tongue, then nibbled on his earlobe, whispering into his ear as he took the rigid piece of flesh deep into his ass again.

"It feels so fucking Good," Joey said, reaching back to fondle Shayne's tight balls.

"I'm in heaven," Shayne said, reaching up to tease Joey's nipples. "So, so good."

Shayne was indeed in paradise. His dream, which had been dragging on and on for what seemed like an eternity, was finally coming true. He was finally in bed, naked and making love to the only man that he wanted. He was in love with Joey Wilde, and now he was fucking him. And it seemed as natural as taking a stroll down Yonge Street.

"I want you to take me from behind," Joey said, climbing from Shayne and positioning himself on all fours. Shayne hurried to comply, burying his cock to the hilt in Joey's tight ass, causing both of them to groan.

"That's it, Shayne. Right there, now rotate your hips. Ream that hole. Oh, fuck."

"I can fuck you all night!" Shayne said through his clenched teeth, his breathing becoming labored.

"Harder! Oh my God, I can feel it in my throat."

It was the first time that the two had sex together, and the anticipation was affecting how it was progressing. No more than thirty minutes in, and both were nearing orgasm. Joey had fallen face-first into the pillow, his cock rubbing against the mattress as he liked to do, his ass still up for Shayne to enjoy.

Flesh slapped upon flesh as they grunted in unison, Shayne being the first to climax, sending blast after blast of hot cum deep into him. Joey was not far behind, and his orgasm rocked him with more intensity than he had ever felt before. As Shayne fell on top of Joey's back, Joey lay shaking with orgasmic spasms still pulsing through him.

With their coupling complete, they lay side by side, reflecting and sharing the experience.

Shayne said, "I would never, in a million years, have guessed that you, of all people, are a submissive bottom. You look so macho."

"How does that song go? I'm a lover, not a fighter. Well, I think that's me. I have never been the aggressive type."

"I see that now. I'm glad that I am versatile. Can you imagine if we were both bottoms?" Shayne laughed.

"I guess that might be a deal breaker, huh?" Joey said, sitting up.

"Deal breaker?"

"Well, I have a proposition for you." He climbed out of bed and grabbed his pants, fishing the wallet out of the back pocket.

Shayne looked on as his curiosity was building. "What are you up to?"

Joey sat back next to Shayne. "Well, I was wondering if you would…might…er, consider maybe moving in with me, if you want to, that is." Joey had rehearsed how he would ask Shayne a thousand times, and still he muffed it, sounding like a young boy asking a girl to the dance for the first time. His face went red with embarrassment.

Shayne just sat there staring at Joey, his mind trying to process what he had just been asked to do. "You want me to move in?"

"Yeah."

"With you?"

"Um, that's the idea." Joey fumbled with his wallet and found the two rings, handing one of them to Shayne.

"What's this?"

"It's a token of our relationship—one for each of us. I hope the inscription fits. It does for me."

Shayne read it then leaped into Joey's arms, kissing him. "Of course, I will move in, and the inscription is perfect." He tried to slip the ring on his finger with difficulty. "It doesn't fit."

"Oops, wrong one. Try this one."

They exchanged rings and both fit perfectly.

"How did you know my size?"

"Claire told me."

"That little minx. She must have looked through my stuff. I love the rings, Joey. Is that a real emerald?"

"Yes. Green is my favorite color."

"Mine too," Shayne said, and they kissed again. "Let's make love again and try to make it last longer this time?"

"You don't have to ask me twice."

Paul hadn't been feeling well over the last few days, fatigue was gnawing at him even with sleeping well and laying off the booze and the drugs. Something was not right.

He began feeling this way on Wednesday night after having sex with the third man of the night at The Barracks, which had reopened a day after being raided by Toronto's finest. No long-lasting harm came from it, and the arrests were more of an inconvenience: all charges were dropped. The owner, however, had to pay a stiff fine. Now things were mostly back to normal.

Paul took a shower and was drying off when he noticed a spot on his leg that had not been there before. It didn't hurt, but he thought it odd because it wouldn't wash off. He remembered what his doctor had told him: "If anything changes with you, come back to the clinic as soon as you can." He wondered if this new spot fell into that category.

Three days later, three new spots appeared, including one on his face. He was afraid, and it was time to see the doctor.

Claire and Danielle had spent the night together at Claire's place and were now having great fun enjoying the following day. Claire called in sick, something she had never done, and went to Center Island Amusement Park. This time, Danielle and I were both soaking wet from the ride.

"Let's go again!" Danielle exclaimed, pushing back her wet hair. "I haven't had this much fun in years!"

The boat jerked as it splashed down, laughter and shrieks echoing over the water as Claire clung to Danielle, the rush of the ride momentarily washing away her lingering anxieties. Spray sparkled in the sunlight, and for a while, nothing else mattered. Danielle squeezed her hand, her smile infectious, and Claire let herself be pulled into the moment, forgetting work, city life, and the silent worries that sometimes crept in at night.

Elsewhere in the city, the late afternoon light slanted through Rebecca McCormick's kitchen window, illuminating dust motes in the air and casting a warm glow over the cluttered table. The quiet of the room was deceptive, hiding the tension brewing just beneath the surface.

She sat at her kitchen table, her eyes red from crying. She was sick and tired of James' lame excuses and didn't buy any of them that he came up with. Did he think she was stupid?

She was far from being an ignorant woman, holding a doctorate in Psychology, and lying to her was not an easy task. Her husband was failing miserably at it. That little weasel was hiding something from her, and if it was the last thing she did before filing for divorce, it was to expose his secret—even if it cost him his job. No one fucked with her and got away with it. If her suspicions were correct, and he was seeing other men, then he would pay—and pay dearly. She picked up the phone, dialed a number from memory, and listened to it ring.

"Canterbury Detective Services. Dave Canterbury speaking. How can I help you?

"Dave, it's Becca. I have a job for you."

CHAPTER 14
First Steps & A Dire Decision

Joey tossed the last bag into the trunk of the Testarossa, leaving no more room for anything else. With Shayne's bags as well as what they had bought during the last three days, the small space was filled. The Ferrari reminded Joey of a Volkswagen Beetle that his father had owned when he was a kid. The trunk was located at the front of the vehicle, whereas the 12-cylinder engine was positioned at the rear. He loved the car.

"Is that everything?" Joey asked as Shayne strolled up and wrapped his arms around his waist. Joey responded by kissing him.

"Yep. I double-checked the room, and there is nothing but our wet towels."

Joey released Shayne from the hug and handed him the keys to the Ferrari. "You drive."

Danielle and Claire sat at a picnic table just outside the amusement park, licking ice cream from sugar cones. Both looked tired after spending most of the day riding every attraction, some more than once. The log flume ride was their favorite, and they went on it six times.

Their clothes, shoes, and hair were wet, matted, and tangled from the water and the day's fun.

"You look like hell," Danielle said, twirling her tongue around the top of the cone. "I'm sure I don't look *any* better."

Claire laughed. "You do, but you still look great to me."

"As do you to me." She said, tossing the napkin wrapped around her ice cream cone into a trash can. "Had enough for one day?"

"Yeah, I'm tired," Claire said, not wanting the day to end as Danielle was suggesting. "I have to work tomorrow, but not until 3 pm, so I have plenty of time to get some sleep."

"I need to be at my office by 9 AM because my client is returning from vacation today. I still need to finalize a contract for him and have it reviewed by a lawyer and the client. Ack!" She was breathless from speaking.

"It sounds like a lot to get done."

"It's not difficult, just time-consuming. Dealing with all of the parties involved is the tiring part. Hopefully, I'll have everything wrapped up by the end of the day."

"We'd better go if we plan on catching the ferry this hour. We have ten minutes." Claire said, looking at her watch.

Danielle stood up, and Claire followed as they both started walking.

Further down the boardwalk, the scent of fried dough and popcorn drifted on the early evening air, mingling with the salt of the sea. The sun hovered low, laughter echoing above the carousel's music.

A gull swooped overhead, bold as ever, snatching the remains of a French fry from a distracted tourist. Danielle caught Claire's eye as she waved, her half-melted cone dripping onto her fingers. Claire giggled, her hair wild and sticking out at odd angles, evidence of their watery adventures.

They jumped onto the ferry just moments before a deckhand was about to secure a chain blocking the entrance. They laughed together and then stood side by side, holding hands as the ferry pulled away swiftly, creating distance from Centre Island as they approached Toronto. Their second date was a success, and as they stood silently, appreciating the scent of the lake, the wind quickly dried their hair. Claire hoped this was only the start.

Paul sat in his doctor's office, bewildered by what he was hearing. He was there because he felt exhausted lately and wanted to understand the dark spots that had appeared on his legs, stomach, and face. It didn't take long for his doctor to diagnose him with KS.

"What the hell is that?" Paul asked. Kapi…what did you say again?"

The doctor, a young man, leaned against the examination table facing Paul, his arms crossed. "Kaposi's Sarcoma. I can provide you with the medical terminology, but I won't: that would take too long and is difficult to understand."

"I'm listening."

"It's cancer, Paul. It probably originated in your lymph nodes or blood vessel cells. Your immune system is weakened and can't fight infections because HIV has severely damaged it, lowering your T-cell count to nearly zero."

Paul looked confused as he tried to understand what the doctor was explaining. "Is there medication for this, um, KS?"

"Yes, but its effectiveness is questionable when you have full-blown AIDS."

"I want to try. I'm young and I don't want to die."

The doctor nodded. "There are medications for both. You'll need to start antiretroviral therapy for HIV, which should help strengthen your immune system. For the sarcoma, there are treatments—chemo, sometimes radiation. We'll coordinate with an oncologist. But the first step is to stabilize your health, Paul."

Paul pressed his palms together, his eyes searching the linoleum floor for answers he wasn't sure he wanted. "So, what now? What do I do next?"

"We'll run more blood tests and get you set up with a specialist. Call someone you trust if you want. This isn't something you have to handle alone." The young doctor offered a tentative, steady smile.

Paul nodded, his mind racing. The world outside the office suddenly felt distant and muffled, as if he were seeing everything through glass obscured by rain droplets and streaks. He wondered who he could call; his lover died from the same disease that he had. He realized that he would be alone in this struggle.

"I need to think all of this through," Paul said, looking out the window at the city through the rainy glass.

"Of course," the doctor replied, picking up a clipboard. "Don't take too long, Paul. Everyday counts, and the sooner we get you on the medication, the better. It's your only chance."

"How long if I don't, you know, take the meds?"

The doctor shrugged again. "Who knows. We are still learning about HIV and AIDS, and I wish I knew more. Six months, maybe longer. It's hard to say how quickly the Sarcoma will spread. Right now, I put you at stage 2, so it's critical to act *immediately*."

Paul nodded and watched the doctor leave. He had a lot to think about, and he did his best thinking at The Barracks. It was time to go there to forget momentarily about KS. The comfort of another man would help him forget, at least for a short time. He also needed to find his dealer: he was out of Ecstasy.

"So, when do you want to move in?" Joey asked. "It's not like you have a lot to move, right?"

Shayne switched lanes to pass a semi that was going too slow. "Right away, I guess. Tomorrow, after I meet with my agent. I have to sign the new modeling contract."

"Ok," Joey said, already thinking about issues that might arise from having a roommate. "Shayne, how do we handle when I have a client over for a treatment? I mean, I can't have you sitting there watching the entire time."

"Why not? That way I can keep an eye on you." Shayne glanced at Joey, grinning.

"Seriously, Shayne. I'm not ready to give up my business."

"I don't see a problem at all. When you have an appointment, I can either stay in the bedroom or go across the street for a coffee or a cocktail until you are done. I have my cell phone, so you can call me when it's over. You don't use the bedroom, do you?"

"Hell no. Only the massage table. Believe it or not, I have offered the futon in the living room, but all of my clients prefer the table."

"See, easy solution."

Joey nodded. "Shayne?"

"Yeah?"

"How old is your JEEP?"

"Seven years old with I think 85,000 miles on it, give or take. Why?"

"I only have two parking spots, so I was wondering what to do with the JEEP. You can't park it on the street. Not in this part of the city. It will get ticketed or maybe even towed."

Shayne was pleased that Joey was bringing up possible problems with his move, as well as the solutions being considered. "I could leave it parked over at Claire's. She has a driveway that is not being used. I'm the only one living there with a vehicle."

"Why don't you just give it to her?"

"What? Are you serious? Just give it to her just like that."

"Sure. You give her the JEEP, and I'll give you the Camero."

Shayne's jaw dropped. "You are certifiable, Joey. That car is worth a lot more than my Jeep. Why give it to me?"

"Because I have the Ferrari, I don't need the Camaro, and we need the parking space. And, because I love you."

Shayne pulled off Yonge Street and headed toward the townhouse.

"Where are you going?" Joey asked.

"Claire's townhouse."

"No, you're not. You're coming home with me."

Shayne glanced at Joey. "Ok, but I at least need to stop and grab clothing for my meeting. Is that acceptable?"

"Ok. I don't want our vacation to end. I'm sorry."

"Don't be." Shayne pulled the Ferrari into Claire's driveway, turned it off, and handed Joey the keys. "I'm not comfortable in underground parking garages."

"*Now* you tell me."

Paul walked out of the rain and into The Barracks with his clothing soaked and his hair plastered to his head. He paid at the front desk for a private room, and the attendant pushed a key and a towel under the glass partition. A buzzer unlocked the door, and Paul walked into the central courtyard, where a lone man was swimming in the pool. He walked by him and down the long hallway to Room 5, unlocking the door and entering it.

He stood in the small, dimly lit room, the hum of the air conditioning mingling with the soft patter of rain against a window blacked out by spray paint. Paul let the towel fall over his shoulders, his mind a blur of half-formed thoughts and uneasy anticipation. The Barracks always felt suspended from time, its anonymous corridors and distant echoes inviting both secrecy and confession.

He set his backpack on the narrow bed, glancing at the faded wallpaper, the mirror on the wall reflecting a tired version of himself. He sat down, the springs creaking beneath him, and allowed his breathing to slow, listening to the faint splash of the swimmer in the courtyard and the occasional sound of a sexual act being performed drifting down the hall.

He felt the ache of distance—not just between bodies, but between moments, between the comfort of old routines and the unpredictability of the night. The room, with its battered furniture and the scent of lemon disinfectant, became a silent witness to his solitude and his longing for hope, which seemed out of reach.

As he took off his wet clothes and draped them over the chair, the sound of footsteps echoed outside his door before fading away. Paul lay back, letting the city's storm settle into background noise as the outside world receded, and he drifted into a memory of his late lover and what had been.

The fear he had felt earlier at the doctor's office had dulled into an ache that refused to go away. His head throbbed with the promise of an oncoming headache. Reaching into his pocket, he found a small plastic baggie. Inside was the promise of salvation, at least for a few hours. He opened it and fished out one of the colorful tablets. He chose a yellow one and popped it into his mouth, then lay back on the bed, staring at the ceiling, waiting for the ecstasy to take effect.

An hour later, he was between two men, one with his cock in Paul's ass, the other forcing his deep into his mouth. He let himself be taken and used, not caring what they did to him. He was numb to it all, be it either the drugs or simply not giving a shit.

One of the men crawled under Paul, reinserting his dick into the tight orifice, the other pushing his 8" cock in next to it. Paul groaned with the feeling of his first time being double fucked, the cocks not fucking in rhythm but to their owners' paces, erratic and haphazard, popping out occasionally, then stuffed back inside.

"Ha! Look at that," One of the men said. "The little twink is bleeding out of his ass."

"It serves him right, Dave. The bitch is teasing us like he did. Fuck him harder."

"I will, Chris."

Chris pounded the petite boy beneath him, not caring if he hurt him or not. He was the Master of this twink, who was the submissive slave.

When both men orgasmed, Chris presented his cock to Paul, who had rolled over, a dazed look in his eyes.

"You got blood on my cock. Lick it off." Chris demanded.

Paul did as he was told, knowing that in the end he would have the last laugh.

CHAPTER 15
Moving Day & Danielle

It was 7 AM when Shayne pulled his new Z28 Camaro into the driveway next to Claire's townhouse and woke her up. As Claire made a fresh pot of coffee, Shayne sat at the kitchen table watching her. If they had been a straight couple, he did not doubt that they would have been married by now. He smiled as she handed him a cup, and he told her what was happening. was happy when Shayne told her he was moving in with Joey and *ecstatic* when he offered her his Jeep. At first, she complained that he didn't need to give her such a lavish gift, but when he told her about the Z28 Camaro Joey was giving him, she threw her arms around Shayne's neck, covering his face with kisses.

"This is so cool, Shayne! You and Joey are a couple. When are you moving?"

"Now. The Camero is out in the driveway, oh, and here is the title and the keys for my…er, your Jeep. I think I took everything out of it. Except for a tape of Madonna. I know how much you love her music, and I can't possibly leave you with no tunes."

"You brat! I do love her! I so want to see her in concert, and I want you to be the one to go with me."

"When the production comes to Toronto, it's a date, ok?"

"Yes. What else are you doing today?" She asked, pouring herself a cup.

"Thankfully, I don't have much to move, mainly clothing. I left a lot of my stuff at my parents' place before heading to Key West. I might pick up a few things, but I'm in no rush. I have a meeting with my agent this afternoon. She's finalized a new modeling gig for me, and it seems to be a big one. I'll let you know more.

Shayne paused for a moment. "You know, I am so lucky to have found Danielle as my agent. She excels in her field. You should meet her sometime."

Claire sat with her mouth open as she put two and two together. "Danielle?"

"Yeah. I think she is a lesbian, and she is a beautiful woman."

"Shayne, I haven't had the chance to tell you yet, but I met someone, and we have been out a couple of times already. And before you ask, yes, we slept together."

"Finally, Kitten! Your first as well. I am so happy for you."

"Shayne?"

"Yeah?"

"Her name is Danielle, and she is a talent agent."

Joey deliberately kept his schedule free, expecting Shayne's move-in. He didn't want the distraction of juggling a client and Shayne at the same time. He planned a special day and their first evening together at home in the condo. To prepare, he washed all the sheets and pillowcases and cleaned the apartment, leaving it spotless for Shayne's arrival.

Unbeknownst to the trio, fate often weaves its threads with a mischievous hand. The realization that Danielle had entered each of their lives in such different, intimate ways left the air humming with possibility. Conversation crackled, the lines between coincidence and destiny blurred as Claire and Shayne exchanged glances—half disbelief, half anticipation. Outside, the city pressed on with its usual indifference, but inside the condo, everything seemed charged, the promise of intertwined stories beginning to unfold.

As the afternoon sunlight filtered through freshly cleaned windows, Shayne's phone buzzed—a message from Danielle. She'd confirmed the address for their meeting. Claire reached for her mug, a smile tugging at the corners of her mouth. "Looks like we're both in good hands," she teased.

Meanwhile, Joey checked his watch his anticipation was building. He set out a tray of pastries and fresh fruit, determined to make Shayne feel genuinely at home. There was a sense of newness, not just in the linens or the sparkling countertops, but in the way their lives seemed poised on the cusp of something extraordinary.

"Hello?" Joey picked up his new landline and answered it. The bills from his cellphone were mounting, so he would advertise the new number in NOW magazine and forward his home phone to his cell when he went out. He wished he could forward the cell, but the option to do so wasn't available. It would at least save him on the incoming calls.

"Hey! I'll be heading to you in about an hour. I'm talking to Claire over coffee."

"Cool. Did she like you giving her the Jeep?"

"She loves it, but it took a bit of convincing for her to accept it. The Camero you gave me made the deal."

"I love you, Joey!" Joey heard Claire on the phone.

"Love you too!" He said back.

"I've got to go. I need to finish up, get home, and change for the meeting with Danielle. Oh, and Joey?"

"What is it?"

"Claire is dating my agent.

After hanging up, Joey stayed by the window, his eyes following the city below. Above the faint traffic noise, he could almost feel the energy of stories unfolding with each passing moment—how Danielle, Claire, and Shayne became part of his world, and how tonight, their connections would grow even stronger.

He began tidying the living room: fluffing pillows, lighting a cedar-scented candle, and playing soft jazz. The music filled the apartment, with the sensual melodies of a saxophone drifting over the deep bass.

Claire's laughter, still echoing softly through the phone, lingered in the air, filling the space with warmth and a touch of mischief.

The minutes passed quietly in a gentle, rhythmic pace. A distant siren sounded and then faded away, while shadows moved across the hardwood, creating shifting mosaics. Joey ran his hand through his hair and looked at the clock once more; his excitement tingled beneath his skin, like an electric current. Soon, the elevator door would open, and a new chapter—untold and full of promise.

Danielle sat in her office sorting through the pages of Shayne's contract, double-checking the numbers and signature that she already had, mainly that of Shayne's new client. The deal changed somewhat, a common occurrence in the fashion industry. Instead of a single shoot, Shayne would now be doing three, all in separate locations. The product was another new release, this time from Coco Chanel. The men's body spray was guaranteed to attract women who wore it. With Shayne's looks and his body, Danielle didn't think that he needed the spray. He was a naturally born chick magnet, even if he was gay.

Danielle tapped her pen thoughtfully against the edge of her desk, her mind weaving through possibilities. There was always a negotiation, always some curveball, but she relished the challenge. As she gathered the documents, her phone buzzed with a new message— Claire's name lighting up the screen. She smiled, their plans for the evening a welcome punctuation to her relentless schedule.

She was suddenly distracted by a soft tap on her door, and it opened, Shayne's head poking through.

"Is it safe?" He asked playfully.

"Come in and have a seat," Danielle said, standing up to greet him.

Shayne shook her hand and they both sat down, Shayne grinning sheepishly at her."

"Ok, what's up with you? She asked.

"I was just wondering."

"What? Spit it out, already."

"I was wondering if it is a conflict of interest. You're dating my best friend, I mean." Shayne was nearly bursting with the joy of letting the secret out.

"Claire is your best friend. I don't believe it."

"We grew up together. She is head over heels with you. You will be kind to her? Please?"

Danielle couldn't believe what she was hearing and quashed any doubts. "I love Claire, Shayne. I haven't felt this way for a very long time. No, I take that back, I have never felt this way about anyone ever. She means the world to me."

"Ok. I don't want to sound like a mother hen. I'm sorry."

"Don't be. I would be asking the same questions if I were you. Now that that is out in the open, can we get to this contract? The job has gotten bigger."

"Oh?"

"Danielle went through it paragraph by paragraph, and an hour later, Shayne left his signature inked onto the crisp pages of the contract. He couldn't wait to get home and fill Joey in, although he had a feeling that he wouldn't be all that pleased.

Outside, rain began to drift in gentle sheets along the office window, blurring the neon lights below and casting the city in a soft watercolor haze. Danielle glanced at her reflection, then at the neat stack of contracts awaiting signatures. Business and life—chaotic, overlapping, and sometimes, unexpectedly poetic. She had put in a long workday yet again and was close to being late for her date.

She slipped everything into her bag and headed out, umbrella in hand, heels clicking a determined rhythm down the marble corridor. Somewhere across town, Claire was waiting. Their worlds were about to entwine again, just as stories do—threads stitched into the fabric of a novel, each character unknowingly writing a following line in the plot.

As the elevator doors closed, Danielle thought of Shayne, of Claire, of the intricate network of friends and clients and chance encounters that colored her days. In their small constellation, everyone orbited each other—sometimes close, sometimes distant, but always within the same night sky.

As Danielle drove toward Claire, she reflected on Shayne and his relationship with Claire. There was nothing more substantial than a best friendship, except for perhaps a romantic one. She hoped as the days progressed that she and Claire's love would build into something unbreakable, bound by trust and friendship.

She pulled into the driveway and parked behind Shayne's Jeep. Claire, she thought, needed a car of her own. She would have to look into it.

"Tell me again, where are they sending you?"

"It's written here in the contract. I'm going to be gone for a month and will come home for two days between two of the shoots."

"That sucks, Shayne. But I understand." But Joey didn't want to understand. He was pissed off and was having a difficult time hiding it. "Key West, of all places. Why there?"

"Jonathan won't be there." Shayne offered. "And it will be all work for the three days at the Pier House. I won't have time to go out, and even if I did, the only person I know there is Travis, and he is probably gone."

Joey stood up and looked out the window. "Where else did you say? After Key West, I didn't hear a thing."

"Paris for four days, then the Algarve in Portugal for four more."

"And you are modeling for who and what?" Joey asked, walking to the sofa and plopping down.

"It's a body spray called Parfum de masculinité by Coco Chanel. You are mad at me, aren't you?"

"No. How can I be? Work is work, and modeling is what you do. How much this time?"

"Twenty-five thousand. For each location."

Joey whistled. "You are raking it in. When do you leave?"

"That's the best part. Not until September, so we have lots of time together until then."

"Fall," Joey said aloud. "At least you will be home for Thanksgiving and Christmas. You will, won't you?

"I plan on it as it will be our first."

"I Learned something else today."

"What is that?"

"My agent is dating Claire."

"No freakin' way! How wild is that?"

"Claire and I made the connection over coffee this morning, and I spoke to Danielle about it as well. I'm very happy for them."

Joey reached over and pulled Shayne onto the sofa, embracing him and kissing him deeply. "I am very happy for us."

Shayne kissed him back and said, "Take me to our bedroom."

CHAPTER 16
A Matter of a Photograph

Things were working out well for Joey and Shayne's living arrangement. Joey continued to his clients, and Shayne had no issues with leaving the apartment or doing something else. The next modeling gig was a small one for a sporting goods company. He would be modeling shorts. It didn't pay much, but it was one more in the pipeline for which he would eventually get paid.

Joey kissed Shayne as he entered the elevator, heading to meet Claire for lunch. He missed her because she was busy with Danielle. Their evening dinners and even a date at Komrads were infrequent. They once tried going to a nightclub with Danielle, but Joey had a double booking and couldn't go. Shayne quickly felt the same way he had in Key West with Sandy—feeling left out. Sandy would often get absorbed in conversations with other girls or get swept away, leaving Shayne alone and ignored. Not intentionally, but it happened too frequently. The feeling of being excluded was terrible, and he usually let them be. He wasn't going through it again in Toronto with Claire. If they went out for the evening, it would be just he and Claire or the four of them.

Joey had another session with Chris, whom he had decided to drop as a client. Recently, Chris had been making advances, which Joey rejected, but Chris either ignored his refusals or didn't care. Joey wondered if Chris saw him as a challenge he wanted to overcome. Joey was done with it. This would be their final session, as he didn't want any more frustration.

"I'm sorry, Chris, but this will be our last session." He had explained. "I am no longer willing to provide you with my services."

Chris had freaked out and begged and pleaded with Joey not to stop seeing him, and that he was sorry if he had said or done something to upset Joey."

Joey had been firm and stood and watched as the elevator door closed, a pleading Chris standing in the middle of it.

He ran his hand through his hair and shook his head, then went to shower, feeling relieved that the ordeal was over.

Chris was stunned as he got into his car, feeling shocked after being dumped by the most beautiful man he'd ever met—though they weren't even dating. It was just a professional breakup between Joey and a client, which was simple enough. Still, it hurt, and Chris felt terrible as he started the engine. He needed to vent his frustration, so he called Paul and scheduled a meeting. That little twink would pay for what just happened. No one messes with Chris Lauden without consequences. He revved the engine and merged onto The Esplanade without looking, and a siren suddenly sounded. He slammed the brakes, hearing a crunch, and looked in the rear-view mirror to see police lights flashing on top of the car he had hit. He groaned, sank back into his seat, closed his eyes, and knew that little shit would pay dearly.

Outside, the day was bruised with a slow-moving rain, washing the city's edges in streaks of silver. Inside David's office, the low hum of fluorescent lights and the faint scritch of his pen were the only sounds as he considered his next steps. The investigation became a tangle of a few photographs, conjectures, and dead ends. Yet his instincts told him there was still more beneath the surface—something connecting these people in ways that weren't yet visible.

He stood behind his desk, looking at a pinboard that hung on the wall. So far, there were only three photographs attached to it, and none of them were inconsequential to his case. One showed the suspect entering Brandy's on The Esplanade, and another showed him entering the bank where he worked. The third had been interesting initially, but after further investigation, the short, chubby kid he had been talking to on the street turned out to be an employee of the bank, not some secret lover. So far, he had been striking out in finding proof for his client that her husband was a homosexual.

The information Rebecca provided about the NOW Magazine ad and the chance of James seeing the massage therapist was thin at best. He thought it was practically impossible. The therapist, a man named Joey Wilde, seemed openly gay and had a partner. Photos of Joey and his lover kissing confirmed this. It didn't prove any relationship between Joey and James. The images with Joey and his partner together suggested that Joey and James were not romantically involved.

He picked up his phone, called his secretary, and had her put in a call. Maybe NOW Magazine had more on Joey Wilde, and he had an in with the editor. Another lead that he had yet to follow up on was Greg Sheske. Joey and Greg seemed to have some professional relationship. Maybe he could garner something from Greg. He just needed to figure out how.

"NOW Magazine, Bob Trench, Editor in Chief speaking. How can I help you?"

"It's Dave Canterbury, Bob. I was hoping you could help me with some information."

James' wife believed his lie that the massage therapist and the ad were for his employee. At least he thought so. Rebecca had been acting like her usual self, so he figured that their argument was settled and resolved. He felt horny and contemplated calling Joey. He could use his stress-relieving hands. The only lingering question was when? He had gotten Joey's number again, this time not ripping it out of the magazine but writing it on a card and putting it in his Rolodex on his desk at work. He gave it the name Jack Timmons of Timmons Heating and Cooling. He believed that the secret card was well hidden. His wife never came to see him at the office.

James had the option to bypass his secretary when making a phone call by simply dialing nine to get an outside line. He reached forward, pressed 9 with his eraser, followed by Joey's number. After two rings, Joey answered.

"Joey Wilde." The voice said through the phone.

"Hi, Joey, this is James. I'm not sure if you remember me."

"Sure. The banker dude."

"Yeah. Um. That's me. I was hoping you would have time to see me. I've been under some stress lately and could use a treatment."

"Of course. When did you have in mind?"

James shuffled through some loose paperwork, pretending to search for something. "Ah, here we are. My schedule is open for tomorrow. Can we set it up for 1 PM?"

"Hold on a sec." Joey reached for his appointment book and flipped to the relevant day. He had another appointment with Joe from downstairs, but it was scheduled for the morning. "You got it."

James ended the call with a surge of nervous excitement. He had repeated his actions, and soon the secret he kept would accumulate more memories. He wondered how long his secret could remain hidden. At that moment, James was indifferent to such thoughts. All that mattered was reconnecting with Joey and feeling the pleasure only his hands could give. Tomorrow could not come soon enough.

"I'm getting sick of you cheating on me." Shayne laughed. "Seriously, though, I miss you. Don't you think you spend too much time with Danielle?"

"Heck no," Claire answered, covering her bagel with a swath of cream cheese. "We don't spend *enough* time together. But get this! Ready?"

"Hit me." He replied, putting lox onto his.

"Danielle has asked me to move in with her. She has a condo, and guess where it is?"

"Ottawa?" Shayne asked, taunting his friend.

"No! Don't be a goof. She lives in the building on the other side of the hotel near you!"

"Oh my God! Don't tell me we are going to be neighbors? Oh, MY God, what is a girl to do?!"

"Can you be serious for one minute, please?"

Shayne calmed down and listened.

"She has a two-bedroom on the 10th floor that overlooks the city. She rented it, but is moving into it, and is selling the other apartment."

"What's wrong with the other apartment. It's on or near Bloor, isn't it?"

"Yeah, but the building is old, and she says that the assessments are murder. Last month, she had to pay $3000.00 for a new pool that she doesn't even use. The condo next door was recently renovated, and the building is about the same age as you and Joey's."

"Joey's. We're not married yet."

She reached over and slapped his arm. "Stop it! I want you to be happy for me. Now we can sneak out for a drink at Brandy's together. Don't you see, the move will allow us more time together. And there is another thing."

"What's that?"

"I've been hired at The Keg Steakhouse and Bar across the street from your building! I can walk to work!"

"This all seems very convenient for you," Shayne said, smiling, not quite ready to be completely serious. "What about Dino's?"

"I put in my notice, and they didn't put up a fuss. I'll make more at the Keg anyway, so I don't care what they might think."

Shayne leaned over and hugged Claire, then gave her a peck on the lips. "I am incredibly happy for you. I think this will be great for everyone. When are you moving?"

"I already did. I sublet the townhouse to my roomie, who will assume the lease once it's up next month. Oh, Shayne, I couldn't be happier!"

The two were interrupted by Joey, who strolled up and sat down. "Well, I just fired a client," he said, taking Shayne's bottle of Diet Coke and taking a sip. "But I got another." He held up the bottle as if to toast.

"Claire has some awesome news as well, Joey. Tell him, Claire."

The rain kept falling, soaking the streets of Toronto with heavy bursts, then easing into a miserable, cold drizzle. David sat in his parked car on the curb outside the Old Spaghetti Factory, which gave him a view of the bank and 25 The Esplanade. He rechecked his camera to ensure the film was correctly loaded and the zoom lens was clean. Finally, he checked the batteries in the motor drive, replacing them just in case he needed to take quick shots in sequence.

He hadn't gained any useful insight from NOW Magazine's editor and decided to monitor both locations where James might go. The bank was certain, but if James entered the 25 building, it could be significant. He checked his watch, which showed 12:50 PM. When he looked up, he saw James exiting the bank.

"Bingo." He aimed the camera and took a few shots. "Late lunch, James?" He said aloud.

James looked up and then down the Esplanade, causing David to slouch down. He then turned and walked toward 25 The Esplanade, David shooting photo after photo until the auto winder screamed it was out of film. James had vanished into the building.

David put in a new roll of film, got out of his car, and hurried across the street after James. He saw him at the end of the hall near the elevators, stepping into the last one.

Once James left, David followed him until he stood in front of the elevator James used. There was no button, only a keypad that needed a code. There was also no indicator over it to tell him which floor James was going to.

"Damn it to hell," David said under his breath. He could follow no further, so he retreated to the front desk.

"Where does the elevator with the keypad go to?" he asked the concierge.

"Penthouses. That last one goes to either PH1 or PH2, depending on the code used."

"You don't happen to know the code, do you?"

"Of course not! The elevator opens directly into the apartment. That code is highly secret and known only to upper management and the owner."

"Thanks anyway," David said and returned to his car. He marked the time James went in; now he would wait. Finally, he had something substantial to report. One thing he did learn from Bob over at NOW Magazine was that Joey Wilde lived at 25 The Esplanade, and his address was listed as PH2.

Across the city, Paul listened to his answering machine, Chris's voice dark and demanding. He sighed, already regretting whatever storm was about to break. He was used to Chris's volatility, but something about the tone warned of fallout more complicated than usual. Paul checked the time, grabbed his coat, and headed out, the rain swallowing him as he stepped onto the street.

CHAPTER 17
Neighbors & Fag Hags

On Saturday morning, sunlight found its way stubbornly through the cloud breaks, glimmering on puddles and the odd green shoot thrusting from sidewalk cracks. From the window of PH2, Joey Wilde watched the city come to life, sipping a mug of coffee and letting the warmth seep into his hands. The view from the penthouse carried a kind of hush, the traffic below muffled and distant, the city's rush made ornamental by altitude and glass.

He woke up before Shayne and planned to make breakfast for both of them, but he got distracted while gazing out his living room window. Having lived with Shayne for nearly a week, everything was going smoothly. Not only was Shayne the love of his life, but he also proved to be an ideal roommate—constantly tidying up and prioritizing Joey's needs. Joey tried to mirror Shayne's habits but often fell short. He tended to leave his dirty clothes on the bedroom floor or discard a wet towel after a shower into the corner of the bathroom, both of which Shayne had caught him doing and then picked up after him. Joey would apologize and promise improvement.

Joey was brought back from his daydream with the embrace from behind from Shayne, who ran his hands over the bare, muscular chest of his lover, lingering to toy with his stiff nipples.

"Last night was incredible," Shayne said, releasing Joey from the hug. "Are you ok? You looked, well, preoccupied when I walked into the room. Is anything bothering you?"

Joey turned back and hugged Shanye, pulling him close. "Everything is better than fine. I'm in love with the most amazing man on Earth, but sometimes I feel I don't deserve him." Joey offered a smile that always made Shayne's stomach flutter.

"And who is this man? Are you cheating on me, Joey Wilde?" Shayne teased, playing along.

"You are that man, and you know something?"

"What?"

"I am going to marry you, that's what."

"You'd better find me a very gaudy and costly engagement ring. I refuse to be outdone by that fag hag Claire."

"Is she getting married to Danielle?"

"I don't think so. At least, not yet. I'm thrilled she finally found someone to love. I didn't mention this before, but I felt tremendous guilt when I went to Key West and later learned Claire wasn't going to University. I probably wouldn't have gone if I had known, Joey. Leaving her alone like that. I was her only and best friend."

"You needed to live your own life, Shayne, and we would not have met. Besides, everything worked out for the best, didn't it?"

"Yes, you're right," Shayne said, walking to the kitchen. "I need coffee."

"I can use a refill myself," Joey said, following him.

"Anything scheduled for today? It's Saturday." Shayne asked.

"I had a regular, the guy from downstairs. You know, Joe, but he cancelled. His mother is sick, so he is driving down to Hamilton for the weekend. I am free for the weekend."

"I thought you had James, or whatever that banker's name is?"

"He was yesterday. Got something in mind?"

Shayne took a cup from a rack on the countertop and filled it with coffee, then poured some into Joey's cup. "Claire mentioned that she was going with Danielle out to Centre Island. Why don't we go with them?"

"It would be fun, and being in the sunshine would be a nice change from all this crappy weather we have been having."

"I'm sick of the rain as well. What time is it?"

Joey checked his watch. "6:30 PM on the dot."

"It's early, but if I know Claire, she is up and raring to go. I'll give her a call."

Joey blew on the steaming cup of coffee he held, watching Shayne go to the phone. "It's cool that she lives next door, now."

"Very cool." Shayne dialed her number from memory.

The Barracks were wrapped in yellow tape that read "Crime Scene Do Not Cross," and emergency vehicles blocked the street. Clark Peterson decided to go to the bathhouse to take a morning swim and do a little cruising when he arrived on the scene. The CEO of Darlington Enterprises wasn't worried about being seen near the gay establishment; it was just another building on a busy street. To anyone who recognized him, he was walking along, minding his own business. His secret was safe.

He stopped, his path blocked by the authorities who were going about their various tasks. A lone police officer stood idly by, seemingly guarding against anyone who would cross the tape. Clark walked up and addressed the officer.

"Looks like a mess. What happened?" Clark inquired.

"Active crime scene inside," The cop said flatly. "It seems that some faggot was strangled sometime last night. The people who clean the place found him this morning."

Clark winced at the use of the cop's word "faggot" but didn't comment on the offensive word. He had more questions, such as who the deceased was, among others, but decided it was best not to pry. A pedestrian passing by would usually not be concerned with the grim details. He walked around the barricade and headed back to his car. He could go to another bathhouse; there were many in the city, and the story would likely be in the Toronto Herald sooner or later. He hoped it wasn't someone that he knew.

Back in his apartment, Clark turned on the news, half-expecting a bulletin to scroll across the screen. Nothing appeared. He took off his jacket, his mind racing through a list of faces, recalling laughter and sideways glances from dimly lit rooms. Was it someone he knew? Or maybe someone he'd passed in the dimly lit tiled hallways? He poured himself a glass of water, the constant hum of city traffic outside serving as a reminder that life continued.

"We can meet up at the Amusement Park." Claire offered, and Danielle quickly nodded in assent. The amusement park became an oft-visited place for the couple's Spur-of-the-moment trips and eventually became the norm.

"I haven't been there in years!" Shayne exclaimed. Is there anything new?"

"Yeah. There is a new ride with a view of the city, as well as a log flume attraction. You'd better be prepared to get wet!" Claire laughed.

"Shorts and sandals it is then. What time do you want to meet?"

"Let's try to catch the 8:00 AM ferry as it's the first one. We can meet at the ticket booth."

"Perfect. Oh, and Joey is wondering if Centre Island is clothing optional."

"Asshole!" Joey threw a dish towel at him.

Claire laughed. "Don't pick on Joey like that. He can still throw you out."

"Don't give him any ideas, Claire. See you both soon."

"What was that?" Joey asked, picking up the towel.

"She said I'd better be nice to you, or you might throw me out."

"That's right!" Joey gave the towel a quick twist and snapped it at Shayne's ass as he quickly retreated toward the bedroom, Joey in close pursuit.

"So, that is where we stand," David Canterbury said to his client over the phone. "James went into 25 The Esplanade at precisely 12:50 PM and exited the building an hour later. And I verified which apartment, as well as who owns the condo, that he went to. One Joey Wilde owns penthouse 2."

Rebecca believed she now had enough evidence to accuse her husband of infidelity with a *man*. The detective agency provided limited details about Joey Wilde: he was probably in his early twenties, worked as a massage therapist from his apartment, was likely gay, and appeared very attractive in the photos shown to her. She did not harbor any resentment towards the man, and if she had been fifteen years younger and he had been straight, her feelings might have been different. She had her revenge planned, and after the divorce, she intended to claim everything she and James owned, as well as any hidden assets he might have. Her goal was to ruin her husband's life in response to his treatment of her and the humiliation she experienced.

"I intend to file for divorce, David. Do we have enough on James?"

"I believe that we do, but just enough. I want to get more. If he has this secret, who knows what else he might be hiding?"

Rebecca twirled the telephone cord around her fingers as she contemplated her next move. "Ok. Let's give it another couple of weeks and see where else the rat might slip up. If nothing else by then, I sue for divorce."

"You got it. Oh, and I have an invoice for you that needs to be brought up to date. Expenses, you understand."

"Gladly. But don't send the physical bill here to the house." She listened and jotted the figure being said down on a pad of paper with no explanation of what it was for. She knew what it was. This was *her* secret.

Chris was in a dilemma. He had gotten rough with Paul, and during a BDSM fantasy, he had strangled him. Not to harm him, as it was part of the sex that they were having. He had panicked when Paul had stopped breathing. Instead of seeking help, he locked the door and ran. He was panicking. Had he just committed murder and left the scene? Indeed, if Paul were dead, then he would have been found by now.

Turning himself in was an option, and Chris considered it carefully. But he wasn't sure if Paul was dead. Was his mind running away from him by assuming the worst? He needed to calm down, maybe take a trip up north for a few days. He could head up to Muskoka for the weekend. He should know more by Monday. So far, there had been nothing on the news about Paul. No news was good news as far as Chris was concerned. He went to his bedroom and began to pack.

"Death by strangulation," a detective said as he reviewed the coroner's report. He was briefing his police chief, who had a press conference scheduled for after the meeting. "We have people of interest that I will get to in a moment. There are many men who visit the bathhouse during the evenings. We believe we have the murder weapon and think that it was a bath towel."

"DNA?" The chief asked, looking over the police report.

"The RCMP lab is testing as we speak. It will take some time."

"Witnesses?"

"Very little, Chief. Some of the men who go there are married and don't want their secrets exposed. Others don't want to get involved and claim they saw and heard nothing."

"Ok, what about the victim?"

"Paul Stenhouse, nineteen years of age, with no known immediate family. He is gay and a hustler by the look of it. We searched his apartment and came up with a clientele book complete with names, phone numbers, and addresses, along with details of what the client wants."

"I presume it's sex."

"Yes, and some of it is out there. Cross-dressing, urination, threesomes, the list goes on. Oh, and BDSM."

"Are there names that correspond to the BDSM clients?"

"Yes, there are six, which we are considering as people of interest, as I had mentioned. We are investigating and will subpoena search warrants if needed. In the meantime, we are going to begin questioning these men."

"Good work, so far." The Chief said, standing up. "Let's go talk to the reporters."

"What do you mean I'm a fag hag, Joey Wilde?" Claire asked as the four bought ice cream cones in the amusement park.

"Well, you are, aren't you? Isn't that what a woman who spends most of her time with a gay man is called?"

"Some women take offense to that term, Joey," Claire said, wrapping a napkin around the sugar cone. The sun was high in the mid-morning sky, and already the day was heating up. Summer was on its way.

"I thought that it was a term of endearment?" Joey asked, taking a lick of his pistachio-flavored ice cream.

Shayne spoke up. "For some women, it is. For example, I call Claire a fag hag at times, but she knows that it is said in love and friendship, not in spite or hatred."

Claire nodded in agreement. "I read that back in the 70s is when the word was first used, and it wasn't meant as a friendly remark. As time went by, gay men adopted it and made it acceptable."

"Why?" Joey asked.

"Well," Danielle answered, "gay men were struggling with fighting for equal rights, and women flocked to their cause in support, both straight and lesbians. The phrase was used in conjunction with the support, and today it is mostly used positively."

"That's how I meant it," Joey said apologetically.

"I know you did," Claire replied and kissed Joey on his cheek. Let's finish our ice cream and hit the log flume ride again."

CHAPTER 18
Rumors & A Break in the Case

"Harder." Joey moaned as Shayne fucked him slowly, rotating his hips for full effect, which was driving his lover crazy with lust.

"You like that, don't you, you little tramp." Shanye's breathing was labored, and he stood over Joey's body, which was bent into a V-shape, offering the best access to his hungry asshole.

"Yes, but please faster." Joey panted.

Their trip to Centre Island had been a monumental success enjoyed by all, and upon returning to PH 2, the couple wasted no time stripping off their damp clothing, leaving a trail of clothing leading to the bedroom, which Shayne would pick up later. Joey was on his back, his legs up and over his head, Shayne thrusting in and out of his gaping hole.

"I'm cramping, let's do it on the bed." Joey climbed onto it face down, offering his bubble butt to his lover.

Shayne didn't hesitate and pushed his 8-inch cock balls deep into Joey, eliciting another groan. "Yeah, baby, that's it. Push back against it. Milk it."

Joey's movements were not only affecting Shayne, but the rubbing of his cock on the sheet it was pressed against was causing the building of Joey's orgasm. "Oh, fuck!" He said through clenched teeth.

Shayne responded to Joey by increasing the pace, his thrusts becoming quicker. Both men were rapidly approaching climax, and it exploded upon them at the same time, Shayne ejecting stream after stream of warm sperm deep into Joey's rectum; Joey's ejaculate covering the bed sheet.

Shayne rolled off of Joey and lay breathing hard, then noticed the spasms still rocking Joey. "You ok?"

Joey rolled over as the last one faded. "Yeah. I've never had that many assgasms before."

"Assgasms?" Shayne asked. He had never heard the term before.

"That's what my EX called them. He said that the prostate has millions of nerves that get stimulated during anal sex and can cause a type of orgasm. Not like when we cum, but more like mini spasms that are super enjoyable."

"Huh," Shayne said. "I've never had one."

"We will have to work on that then, won't we?" Joey leaned over and kissed his partner.

"I think that we will. Now, let's get showered and dressed. We are meeting Claire and Danielle across the street for dinner, remember?"

"I remember. I was the one who suggested it, and that I would pay for it.

"The good Samaritan that you are."

Still smiling from their laughter, Shayne got up and headed to the bathroom, where the sound of running water soon filled the apartment. Joey followed, grabbing fresh towels and playfully tossing one to Shayne. They talked about the evening ahead, friends, and stories yet to come, with the anticipation of dinner merging with their post-intimacy glow. After their showers, they dressed in the warm, golden dusk light, preparing to go out and welcome the night with open hearts and eager appetites.

Chris kept switching the radio station in his car, searching for updates about Paul, but so far, there was nothing much to his relief. Driving north on the 400, he felt anxious and nervous, as if his life was spiraling out of control into a dark, ominous place. He packed three suitcases for a two-day trip, which made him question his motives. What if he *had* killed Paul? Would he run from what he'd done? The suitcases in his trunk seemed like proof of his intention to do so. The truth was, Chris was unsure of the right course of action. Right now, he was fleeing—fleeing from himself and what he had become and, possibly, a crime. He checked into that gay guest house advertised in NOW Magazine and tried to relax and figure out his next move.

Chris pulled into a gravel drive lit by a lone porch bulb and the promise of anonymity. The guest house named The Frolicking Frog stood quiet, ivy climbing the old brick, flags fluttering gently in the dusk in front of it. He killed the engine and sat, breathing in the unfamiliar air, letting the tension unwind itself slowly. He had no answers yet—about Paul, about himself—but for now, there was a room waiting, a bed made up by a stranger, and the hush of possibility. He gathered his things, stepped into the silent foyer, resolved to take the night moment by moment, letting himself disappear into the background.

As he lay on the bed in his room, somewhere between the city's laughter and the country's hush, images of books lined themselves up in Chris's mind, each title a door to another world. He wondered which story might hold the key to his peace, which novel or chance encounter would teach him how to be found again.

David was precise in uncovering others' secrets, especially when it involved James Worthington. He was more dedicated to this case than any other; he had an ulterior motive. David Canterbury harbored a secret: he was in love with Rebecca, and he had been since their first meeting at a local business gala. James and his wife had attended, and during a chance encounter while getting a glass of punch, David was captivated by the younger brunette. Rebecca was twenty-three at their first meeting, and a friendship blossomed between them. Over time, they became close friends, though David secretly desired more. He kept his feelings hidden, knowing he would not be able to convince her to leave her husband for him, and had never even suggested the idea. Her loyalty to James was widely recognized and accepted within the circles of both of their lives. Now, however, circumstances had changed. She intended to divorce James, which would leave her single and available. Blowing this case wide open would give him the chance that he desired—intimacy with Rebecca Worthington.

His opportunity arrived on a Saturday afternoon when David was surveilling the bank. With his two-week deadline from Rebecca nearing, he needed to gather more details about James' activities outside of work and home. Earlier, she had called him, saying James mentioned he was heading to work to finish some paperwork before Monday. She also said James had been acting strangely, raising her suspicions. Seizing the moment, David hurried to the bank and waited in his car. He saw James arrive and enter the building, but he didn't see him leave. Two hours later, that would change.

James needed a change of pace away from his frigid wife, who was becoming impossible to be near for any length of time. Joey was not available, so he thought he might try one of the many bathhouses that Toronto had to offer. Most were located around the Church and Wellsley area, so he would take a cab to one of them, leaving his car in the bank's parking garage.

James had been reflecting on his meetings with Joey lately, and his latent homosexuality appeared to be intensifying the more he thought about it. Having any sexual encounter with his massage therapist was out of the question, as Joey had made it clear there would be no sex between them except for the happy ending hand job. James needed another plan, and the gay bathhouses seemed the easiest course of action to explore new areas of his sexuality. And it would be anonymous, which was to his liking as an unhappily married man. His first attempt was going to The Barracks one morning, but police activity had turned him away. He had left quickly, not wanting to be seen or involved in what was going on in and around the bathhouse. That day, he had returned home frustrated. This day, he hoped, would be different.

James had gone into the bank to finalize a contract he had neglected to finish before the end of the week; that part of what he told his wife was genuine. He omitted his plans for when he was finished with the work. He checked his messages and found none, locked his office, and left, nervousness invading his stomach. He went in search of a cab to hail.

David saw James immediately when he exited the bank and watched as he waved his arm in an attempt to hail a cab. "Why the cab?" David said aloud, starting his car. James had driven his vehicle to the bank, and he had seen him drive it into the garage.

James climbed into the back of a yellow taxi as David pulled into traffic. He followed James through the city as it made turns onto streets that David guessed were meant to throw off anyone who might be following him. David, being a seasoned detective, was not fooled and kept two cars behind the taxi.

A few minutes later, the cab pulled into a side street, and James climbed out, handing the driver a folded bill. David snapped a few

Photos, adjusting the zoom lens, then watched as James crossed the street, glanced around, and entered a door, disappearing. Looking up, David read the sign and smiled. It read 'Recreation Spa' in neon lights that blinked, needing repair.

He grabbed a duffel bag from the back seat, as well as a small camera designed to look like a cigarette pack, parked his car, and followed James inside. By the time he had arrived at the check-in desk, there was no sign of his suspect.

"Can I help you?" A young man asked in a very feminine manner, looking over David from head to toe, not trying to hide his interest. The man, who looked no more than a teenager, stood behind a glass partition and was the desk clerk.

"Maybe. I'm supposed to meet a friend here. He's about my height with blondish hair and wears glasses. Has he come in yet?"

"A guy just came in that matches that description. He's inside."

"Can I go see him?" David asked.

"Sure, that will be $45.00 unless you want a private room." The man said slyly.

"No, just the basic thank you." He replied, taking out his wallet and fishing out the money. "There you are."

The clerk took the cash, then pushed a towel and a key under the glass. "Lockers are down the hall to the left," he said and pressed a button that released the door, allowing David to enter.

For the first time in his life, David entered the unknown, which was a gay men's bathhouse, and he knew nothing of what happened within its walls. He could hear telltale signs of sex being performed throughout, although he had yet to see any of the activity firsthand. With the cigarette pack camera at the ready, he walked toward the locker area.

"The Barracks is still an active crime scene and remains closed to the public," the police chief told the media. "Before proceeding, I want to introduce myself and a respected colleague. I am Mathew Baxter, Chief of Police for the Metro Police Department. To my right is Tom Hussley from the Royal Canadian Mounted Police. The RCMP, as some may know, is often called in for murder cases, and we appreciate their support. We have confirmed that Paul Stenhouse was murdered on Thursday evening. We are currently locating and questioning a few persons of interest, whose names we are not releasing at this time for obvious reasons. No arrests have been made yet, and we don't believe the public is in danger. I want to emphasize that there is no threat to the community. We also suspect this was likely the work of a single suspect. With that, I'll take a few questions." The chief finished, then pointed to a woman sitting in the front row of the media room.

"Does the RCMP's presence have anything to do with this being a homosexual murder and the gay portion of the city?" She asked.

The RCMP officer stepped forward. "The RCMP investigates crimes that could involve areas outside of where they were committed."

"So, you think the murderer may have fled the city?" Her follow-up question was directed toward the Chief.

"Anything is possible, but there is no evidence of such," he answered, stepping forward. "I called the RCMP to assist if such a situation exists. Then, the RCMP would take a more active role in the investigation. As of now, they are helping with the forensic evidence we obtained from the crime scene."

Another reporter stood up. "It is rumored that this was a gay hate crime. Can you expand on that?"

"There is no evidence that a hate crime was committed in this case. Don't believe rumors, Danny."

A chuckle ran through the room.

The meeting continued for another 30 minutes, with the same questions being asked in various ways, each being answered accordingly. After the meeting, the media were frustrated as there was little to report to their bosses. As Chief Baxter had repeatedly said, "It was an ongoing investigation."

Back in the Chief's office, the talk had taken a turn with new evidence coming to light, and it was sitting on his desk when they walked into the room. Detectives eliminated five of the six persons of interest, leaving just one, and he was nowhere to be found. Chris Lauden had been seen at The Barracks on the night of the murder, and it had become known that he was into BDSM. The clue that tied him to the murder was that his name appeared in Paul's client book, and next to his name, Paul had written a single word: "Dangerous?"

The RCMP was now an active player in the investigation as the search of Chris's apartment revealed the hurried packing that he had done, leaving the dresser drawers partially empty and open.

Chief Baxter reached for his phone. "Issue an arrest warrant for Chris Lauden. Make it an APB and send it out to the surrounding municipalities ASAP." He hung up and looked at Tom. "We know who, but where? He has a good head start."

"I'll get on the horn. We will get him. He can't run forever."

"I'd better notify the FBI as well. He might have crossed the border by now." Baxter reached for the phone once again. He could feel a headache coming on.

CHAPTER 19
Evidence & Finality

Danielle and Claire danced together, whirling around the floor of Komrads, lost in the moment, the music of Tainted Love driving them on. When the song blended into another, Danielle led Claire off the floor and to a bar located in the rear of the club, which provided a more intimate atmosphere away from the relentlessly pounding music that dominated the dance area. Danielle could take only so much and needed a break. Claire was grateful to enter the quietness of the outdoor bar as well.

They found a table at the far end of the room overlooking the street below, separated only by a steel railing. Claire smiled at her lover as she walked to the bar to get fresh drinks. While she was gone, Claire had time to think about the last couple of weeks. A new place to live, a new girlfriend, and a new job all topped the list of things that occurred in a very short time. She had never been happier in her life than she was at that moment. She had Shayne back and a new friend in Joey, and now Danielle, who seemed to stop at nothing to please Claire. Sometimes she did feel worthy of the attention that she was receiving and had mentioned it, but Danielle would hear nothing of it. Claire was her soul mate, and she would be treated as such.

"Two Pearl Harbors on the rocks," Danielle said, placing them on the table. Outside, a neon sign reflected on the blue-green liquid, changing the colors of the glasses into a mix of reds and purples. "Where did you learn about this drink?"

"Joey. He found out about it in an outdoor garden bar at The Copa in Key West."

"The Copa? I've been there. It's a really cool nightclub, and the garden bar is gorgeous. There was a bartender who tended to me there. I remember him because he was extremely friendly and appeared to be of Middle Eastern descent. What was his name? Oh, yeah. It was Patrick." Danielle paused and stirred her drink. "That was three years ago. He probably isn't there anymore."

"Ask Joey when you see him. He was just in Key West not long ago. I remember him saying that the garden bar was one of his favorite places to hang out."

"Maybe I will." Danielle thought some more, gazing at Claire with her deep brown eyes. "You are beautiful, Claire, and I love you so very much."

"I love you too."

"Why don't you take a vacation this winter, and we can go to Key West together? I want to go back, and you have never been."

"Shayne and Joey talk about all the good things they did together. Neither wants to talk about their Ex."

"Can you blame them? I wouldn't either. Breakups are ugly and not to be remembered for any reason as far as I am concerned."

"I guess not," Claire said, fiddling with her straw.

"What do you say we get out of here. Let's go for a coffee before we head home. Maybe even a pastry?"

"Yummy, I'm in."

The two finished their drinks and left.

Chris sat in his room at the Frolicking Frog staring at the TV. The latest news briefing was being held and broadcast about Paul's murder and the whereabouts of the man who committed it. Chris Lauden was suspected of strangling Paul Stenhouse at a gay bathhouse and was apparently on the run. An arrest warrant had been issued, and the RCMP was on the case. Lauden was considered dangerous and should not be approached. Inform authorities if you see him. Chris put his head in his hands.

He had checked in under an assumed name with the promise that he was to be joined by his lover in a day or two. He had paid cash. Now he wasn't sure any of it mattered. It wouldn't be long before a photo of him was splashed across newspapers as well as the TV, or at least a sketch if they couldn't find one. Chris had never liked having his picture taken. Luckily, Ontario did not require a picture on its driver's licenses, unlike some other provinces, such as Alberta, where Chris was from. He had surrendered his Alberta license for an Ontario license four years ago when he moved to the city. It would take some digging by the police to find the old permit.

Chris's head was pounding, and he was terrified of what might happen once he was discovered. He did not want to spend the rest of his life in prison. Fleeing to the U.S. from Canada was also not an option, as the RCMP was actively searching for him, and the FBI likely already knew. Chris was running out of options, and despair consumed him.

He unzipped a suitcase and searched through it until he found a small baggie that contained several pills varying in color but otherwise the same. He had taken it from Paul before he fled the room at The Barracks. Why, he couldn't remember, but he knew what they were. Paul took them when he had sex. They were Molly's or Ecstasy, a powerful synthetic drug that altered the mind, causing euphoric effects.

Chris climbed onto the bed and sat with his back against the headboard, staring at the baggie and its contents. The wine that he had been drinking had given him a slight buzz and was also the cause of his headache. He opened the baggie and grabbed the wine glass. With two quick motions, he swallowed the pills and washed them down with the wine. His grief overwhelmed him at what he had done. He could only imagine the terror that Paul had felt before he fell into unconsciousness. He lay back, closed his eyes, and waited for the pills to take effect.

David stealthily moved down the hallway until he saw the lockers—two rows lining each side of the wall and larger closets in the center of the room. He heard moaning coming from one of them. The room was dimly lit, but he could see James wrapping a towel around his waist before closing and locking a locker to secure his clothes. He slid the key, held by a thick rubber band around his wrist. He walked toward David, who quickly turned and pretended to be adjusting the locker in front of him. James walked by him, oblivious. David followed, being careful to stay in the shadows, waiting for the chance for the photo that would seal his case.

Dinner with Joey and Shayne was a pleasure, and Danielle suggested continuing on to Konrads to dance. Joey graciously declined, citing an appointment in the morning. Joe, back in town, had booked an early treatment since he wasn't expected to return to work at the bank until the next day. Claire had begged for Shayne to go, but he knew all too well the probable outcome from such a venture. He would be cabbing it home early, feeling dejected and alone, when the two girls slipped off together as they undoubtedly would. He politely declined as well. An evening with Joey would be perfect. Maybe they could find an old movie to watch.

"Would you ever consider going back to Key West? For a visit, I mean." Shayne asked as they walked to the elevator.

"I haven't considered it, why?"

Shayne shrugged. "I've been thinking about Sandy lately. I miss her."

"Me too. I wonder if we can get in touch with her. We can at least try to call."

"I don't have her number," Shayne said dejectedly.

"I do." Joey smiled and punched the security code into the pad next to the elevator. The door slid open, and he stepped inside, followed by Shayne.

"What do you mean by 'I do.'" Shayne asked. "Where did you get it?"

"She gave it to me before I went to Iowa with JJ. She said it was her parents' number in Illinois, and if I ever needed a lawyer, her dad was the best. She wrote the home number on the back of his business card. I have it upstairs."

"All this time you had the means to get in touch with her and didn't tell me?!"

"You never asked," Joey said, walking into the living room.

"I have half the mind to make you sleep on the couch for a month, Joey."

"Are you pissed off, Shayne?"

"I'm certainly not happy at the moment."

"Calm down. I'll find that card for you, okay? Honestly, I never thought about it. I didn't even discover you until after I moved here." Joey went into the bedroom, leaving Shayne fuming but calming down. He could never stay upset with Joey.

"Found it," Joey called from the bedroom and then appeared holding a business card in his hand.

"What if she isn't there?" Shayne was nervous.

"Then, we talk to whoever answers the phone, tell them who we are, and we would like to get in touch with her. The worst-case scenario would be that they would take the message and relay it to Sandy. Simple."

"What if no one answers?"

Joey took Shayne by the arm and dragged him to the phone, handing him the receiver, then the card. "Now call."

Chris Lauden was found dead in his room by the Frolicking Frog's cleaning staff just before the RCMP arrived at the guest house. One of the owners, DeeDee, recognized him immediately after seeing the news on TV. His appearance matched that of the murder suspect. The news aired just after breakfast, and she called the number on the screen right away. Soon after, a chambermaid informed her about discovering the body. DeeDee quickly realized it was the person they had been searching for upon seeing the body. She secured the room by locking the door, leaving everything untouched, and then went outside to wait for the police.

The cause of death was officially listed by the coroner as suicide by an overdose, a combination of Ecstasy and alcohol, and the case was quickly closed. Many gay people believed that the murder had been pushed under the rug as if it had never happened. This infuriated gay rights activists who championed AIDS awareness. They could have used the tragedy to highlight the dangers of the bathhouses, not necessarily the murder itself, but of the risks of spreading HIV. The victim had been reported to have AIDS, and at the time of his killing, was not practicing safe sex. His rectum was full of the killer's semen. Chris had been infected and never knew it. The entire ordeal was yet another tragedy that would slowly disappear and become another secret, one of many that the city kept hidden. In the end, the faces of Paul and Chris would fade, forgotten by those who had crossed their paths, except for a few who would trace their HIV infection back to them.

Rumors of the story persisted in select circles, surfacing when shadows lengthened and the atmosphere thickened with memories. For some, the names Chris and Paul became cautionary tales— haunting echoes in late-night talks, symbols of love, danger, secrecy, and loss. Still, the city advanced, its streets absorbing secrets as effortlessly as footsteps. New faces appeared, lives intertwined, and the past was relegated to dust in abandoned guest houses and quiet hallways. Even these people would forget, and Chris and Paul would not become martyrs.

Stories tend to endure, often appearing unexpectedly hidden among the worn spines of used books or in the margins of journals written by those who hold onto too much. For every secret kept buried, another story is ready to emerge, subtle yet persistent, gradually becoming part of the city's rich history.

David's persistence finally paid off. He caught James in the embrace of another man, both naked, standing in the doorway of a room. The light wasn't great, but the camera was designed to shoot in dimly lit spaces, as the aperture was set up to let in as much light as possible. David took about a dozen photos, each as incriminating as the last, before he left the two, retreating into the dark hallway and eventually stepping out onto the street. He needed to get the pictures developed and make a phone call.

CHAPTER 20
Exposure

Shayne's major modeling assignment was still a few months away. Meanwhile, Danielle continued to find him occasional jobs, keeping his 'pipeline' active and ensuring a steady income. He offered Joey some money to help cover bills like electricity and rent, but Joey declined, insisting he could easily afford the condo's minimal costs. He pointed out that the maintenance fees covered cable TV, water, and sewer. Living at 25 The Esplanade offered additional perks, including access to a fully equipped gym, a swimming pool that Joey frequented almost daily, tanning beds, security, and their semi-private elevator. Joey paid the monthly fee that covered it all. Shayne had his cell phone to pay for, and as Joey knew all too well, it could be expensive, exceeding $500.00 a month. Shayne made up for it by buying the groceries, beer, and wine, and kept the liquor cabinet fully stocked.

He went out in the morning because Joey had a client arriving for a treatment. His first stop was a salon, where he got his hair cut and styled, along with a manicure and pedicure, since he had a small photoshoot the next day. The salon was one of his favorite activities, and he thoroughly enjoyed the entire experience, which lasted over two hours.

The morning unfolded with gentle promise: sunlight filtering through the high windows, the city's hum muffled by the thick glass. Shayne left the salon with a sense of renewal, admiring his freshly cut hair in every passing reflection. kept it short when he was in Key West, but now he was letting it grow, and it fell onto his collar. He wandered into a small café tucked between a florist and a travel agency, ordered coffee and a croissant, and spent an hour with his sketchbook, mapping out poses and outfits for the coming shoot. The comfort of routine wrapped around him; each small indulgence—an extra shot of espresso, a new tube of moisturizer from the boutique—seemed a quiet celebration of his life.

As the morning waned, Shayne strolled along the waterfront, eyes drifting over sailboats and sun-streaked ripples. When he returned home, the scent of eucalyptus drifted from Joey's living room, a reminder that another of Joey's clients had been there. Joey was not there, and he assumed he had gone for his morning swim. Shayne left a note—back for dinner, won't be long—before heading out again to meet Danielle at a dimly lit bistro. They discussed next steps, new contacts, and the uncertain but exhilarating arc of his modeling career.

Late that evening, Shayne was sleeping in the bedroom. Joey sat in the living room, sifting through a pile of past issues of NOW Magazine, searching for something but unsure of what. The city's secrets pressed close in the dead of night, and he wondered how many stories, like those of many of his clients, lay hidden in the shadows—waiting for the correct page to be turned.

He returned the stack of magazines to a wooden crate beside the sofa, then stood and yawned. In the bedroom, he paused to observe Shayne sleeping peacefully, wondering what his lover might be dreaming. He smiled, undressed, and slipped under the covers, gently embracing Shayne from behind. This elicited a soft murmur from Shayne. The man then closed his eyes, surrendering to sleep as his dreams beckoned.

Claire and Danielle had their first argument, and it had left Claire crying and Danielle storming out of their apartment, fuming. The spat had escalated into an argument over money, not dissimilar to the conversation that Joey and Shayne had, although they had not argued. Claire and Danielle's disagreement had arisen from a conversation that Claire had had with Shayne. They discussed their mutual desire to contribute more financially to their relationships. Neither of them wanted to feel as if they were being 'kept'. They had agreed to discuss sharing more of the daily living expenses with their partners as soon as they had the opportunity.

Shanye had resolved his quest peacefully because Joey acquiesced to letting him buy the groceries and alcohol. Danielle had not considered that possibility and insisted on paying all the monthly condo fees, which sparked an argument that had deteriorated into a name-calling match.

"I'm not your fucking doll to be kept and played with at your leisure!" Claire had yelled. "I have responsibilities too!"

"Not in this house you don't." Danielle argued. "It is my responsibility alone to pay for this condo. It's mine, after all, not yours!"

"I don't want your stupid condo. All I want is to help in its upkeep."

"No, and that is final!"

"Fuck you then. Maybe I should move out."

"Maybe you should."

Danielle left, slamming the door behind her, leaving Claire crying on the couch as she tried to process what had just happened. She only wanted to be more involved and responsible in their relationship. Currently, Danielle covers all expenses, including outside activities like trips to Centre Island, dining out, and ferries. Claire, exhausted by this, finally attempted to pay for something herself, but Danielle often stepped in to cover the costs. She grew tired of this pattern.

She showered quickly and called Shayne. She needed a friend. Luckily, he was available, and she would see him over at his condo.

It never ceased to amaze her every time she took the elevator to Joey and Shayne's apartment and stepped into their living room. She found Shayne chatting with Joey, sitting on the sofa, sipping tea.

The moment Claire entered, Shayne greeted her with his trademark lopsided smile, and Joey offered her a mug of chamomile tea without asking. Something was soothing about the familiarity of their place— the scattered books on the coffee table, the faint scent of sandalwood, the woven throw draped over the back of the couch. She curled up in the armchair, tucking her knees under her, and accepted the tea with a grateful nod.

Shayne glanced at her, concern flickering in his eyes. "Rough day?" he asked gently.

Claire smiled weakly. "You could say that."

Joey excused himself to the kitchen, letting the conversation settle between Claire and Shayne. The city lights outside their window danced in the dusk, casting fractured patterns on the hardwood floor. Shayne waited, letting the silence stretch comfortably.

"It's Danielle," Claire finally said, her voice barely above a whisper, as if speaking the name might shatter her resolve. "Everything feels like a transaction lately. I'm tired of being… taken care of. I want to contribute. I want to matter."

Shayne nodded, understanding in his gaze. "You do matter. To Danielle, to us. Maybe she doesn't know how to let go of the reins."

Claire chuckled humorlessly. "That's putting it mildly."

The kettle in the kitchen whistled, and the scent of lemon and honey mingled with the air. Joey returned, carrying a plate of shortbread cookies, quietly placing them on the table. For a while, they sat together, not as people burdened by the weight of fractured relationships, but as friends, sharing the comfort of quiet company.

As the evening deepened, the conversation drifted toward lighter topics—old books, favorite movies, stories from their shared past. It was here, nestled in the warmth of the living room, that Claire could almost forget the sting of earlier arguments, finding solace in the laughter and gentle chiding of friends who knew her best.

After a couple of hours, Claire excused herself with a fresh resolve to return home and resolve the conflict between her and Danielle. Joey's solution seemed practical, and hopefully her partner would agree to it.

The first thing Claire did upon returning to the apartment was to apologize and make peace, which Danielle was quick to accept and reciprocate. She had been thinking about the situation while sitting at the bar in Brandy's, and came to a similar conclusion. Claire did need to take more responsibility in their relationship, but paying for the condo fees was not the solution. That was Danielle's responsibility, and it was partially tax-deductible since she claimed one of the spare bedrooms as another office space. Claire's solution was both brilliant and amicable.

Danielle agreed that Claire would start paying for groceries and their bar supplies, and she would also begin sharing half of their expenses when they go out in the city, within reason. If they took the trip to Key West as discussed, Danielle would cover most of the costs, while Claire would pay for other expenses, such as dinners and activities they might do.

The two sealed the agreement with a night of passionate lovemaking followed by a night of blissful sleep, Claire dreaming of what Key West might be like.

With photographs in hand, David entered a bistro on the corner of Bloor and Sherbourne Streets, far from The Esplanade and the bank where James worked. He didn't want to risk a chance encounter as he was about to meet Rebecca, James's wife.

He found her sitting in a dark corner at the back, a martini glass in front of her. She wore a veil that partially obscured her face, and David couldn't help feeling that he was entering a scene from a spy novel, full of intrigue and suspense.

Rebecca glanced up as David approached, her eyes flickering with recognition and guarded curiosity. He slid into the seat opposite her, placing the envelope onto the table, letting it rest between them. For a heartbeat, the air was tense, thick with the secret of what the envelope contained. Rebecca broke the silence first, her voice low but unwavering. "You said you had something to show me, new evidence against my husband, James?"

David nodded, fingers brushing the edge of the envelope. "I have the proof that you need. There is enough in this to prove beyond a doubt what you have believed all along." He pushed the envelope across the table, and the din of the bistro faded, leaving only the hum of the overhead lights and the sharp clink of Rebecca's ring against her glass.

She opened the envelope, removed the images, and studied them in silence, her expression unreadable. Finally, she closed her eyes, letting out a breath that sounded like surrender. "Thank you for coming," she said, voice softer now, tinged with something neither relief nor regret. "This will be more than enough to file for divorce and make him pay for what he has done to me.

For a while, they spoke in halting sentences, navigating the fragile bridge between betrayal and understanding. Outside, the city glimmered with the rising sun, a promise of another day filled with challenges and questions yet to be answered. Rebecca Worthington had her answers, and as her soon-to-be ex-husband's secret had been exposed, his life would soon be in turmoil with scandal. She would see to it. David finally rose to leave. There was a tentative agreement between them—a shared knowledge that, while the truth could wound, it could also set them free. David went with the hope that a relationship between him and Rebecca might finally have a chance.

The story broke the following day, Rebecca having contacted the editor of NOW Magazine, and why not, she thought. Let the very tabloid that had started the ruination of her marriage be the downfall of her husband's reputation and career. The magazine published a few of the photographs taken by David as well, partially blurred to hide the other man's face and their genitals. The caption above the two-page article read 'Scandal and a Fall from Grace: Prominent married banker caught in local gay bathhouse with lover resigns position.'

Rebecca had not been at home when James moved out of their $ 1.5 million condo. She was at her lawyer's office preparing her case against James and filing for divorce.

Shayne hung up his cell phone and leaned back, smiling. He left PH2 alone, giving Joey the space to be with another client, and strolled around until he found a nearby bistro close to the harbor in the Distillery District—one he had never visited before. He finally managed to talk to Sandy for a good while, catching up over coffee and a bagel. She returned to Illinois after spending a month in Hawaii. Between jobs and with plenty of free time, she was also short on money.

Shayne updated her on everything that had happened, including finding Joey, their whirlwind romance, and his subsequent modeling career. He invited her to visit Toronto and offered to lend her money until she found a job. She accepted eagerly. Shayne intended to talk to Joey later that day to finalize the details.

As he gazed into his coffee mug, he realized how much he missed Sandy, much more than he thought. Memories of their time together in Key West before Joey appeared flooded his mind in waves, reminding him of over a year of shared moments. He smiled as he picked up the mug, took a sip, and placed it back on the table. He felt his life coming full circle, having evolved from a boy seeking himself through travel to a man with a career, a husband, and extraordinary friends. Grateful for what he had and what he didn't, he was content— without regrets or secrets weighing him down. He felt truly free and alive. He left the mug half empty and the bagel uneaten, and he headed home.

CHAPTER 21
Secrets

At 1 AM, Joey sat with a cup of tea as the city below shone silently—a fabric of secrets he'd never fully uncover, yet others shared through his clients that haunted him. All of them harbored secrets, and for reasons Joey couldn't explain, they chose to confide in him. Common themes included troubled marriages, new revelations about homosexuality and attraction to men, and their uncertainty about the next steps. One client even confessed to embezzling from his company, which helped him afford his sessions with Joey.

Joey pressed the rim of the mug to his lips, the tea long gone cold, but he didn't mind. He was lost in reverie, the kind that only arrived at this hour, when the world was quiet and the past could be examined without interruption. He let most of the confessions pass, trying to ignore what was being told to him, but they always seemed to find a way through, attaching themselves to Joey's mind and memory like unwanted baggage.

He wondered if Shayne was still awake: thoughts of him tiptoeing the floors of their apartment, or sitting at the kitchen table with a notebook, plotting out another photo shoot, or scribbling a letter to Sandy. Their lives had become a tapestry of intersecting threads—love, ambition, woven through without secrets, all confessed, none still held close.

Tonight, the silence felt almost sacred. Joey's mind drifted to his origins—how far he'd traveled from the simplicity of being unable to be himself in Maine to an uncertain life in Key West, which ended with a heartbroken boy arriving in Toronto, unsure of his next step. The city lights blinked back at him as if acknowledging his presence. He remembered the first time he stood at that exact spot in his condo, gazing out, contemplating his future and what might lie ahead. Deep inside, he had sensed a cautious hope blossoming—a belief that what is broken can be repaired, that forgiveness is within reach, and that sharing secrets with the right person could lighten the burden.

Then he had met Claire, who became his first friend in the City, and his reunion with Shayne culminated in what he now considered marriage.

Sandy, a close friend, re-entered his life. He found it amusing how life seemed to circle around a person, believing that, through some kind of magic, the people he needed most would suddenly appear like characters from a haunted novel—ready to help and mend a fractured life. Joey saw it as a two-way process. Shayne wasn't exactly stable when they first met outside The Horseshoe. He had a promising career but an unremarkable social life. Joey changed that and became the missing piece for Shayne, helping him become whole again.

They had suffered at the hands of others, and both swore never again to submit themselves to such heartache, whether by chance or due to their actions. Joey would not do anything to harm his relationship with Shanye, and he knew in his heart that Shanye felt the same.

The hour grew later, the city's glow dimming as the hush of early morning crept across the skyline. Joey's thoughts wandered in and out of memory, the present moment frayed by the weight of stories entrusted to him—ghosts, in a sense, that followed him from session to session, from dusk to dawn. He pressed his forehead to the cool glass of the window, letting his breath fog the view, as if to blur the line between the outside world and the tangle of feelings within.

He wondered if everyone carried secrets the way that he did or if he was alone in feeling haunted by all that had gone unsaid. The city below, vast and impersonal, seemed to hum with the secrets of a million souls, each one hoping for forgiveness or to be understood. Joey traced a circle on the windowpane, thinking of forgiveness—not just the kind extended to others, but the kind he had learned to grant himself.

A distant siren wailed, bringing him back to the now.

He picked up his empty mug, turning it in his hands, and smiled softly. Life had not delivered what he once expected, but in ways both strange and beautiful, it offered him moments of redemption and a sense of belonging. He thought again of Sandy's impending arrival, the intricate pattern of lives intersecting, old chapters reopening, new stories waiting to be told.

Outside, the city seemed to pause, holding its breath for the coming day. Joey let the silence fill him, then exhaled, feeling—at least for tonight—at peace with the secrets he kept for others, and those he had finally let go for himself